CW01149398

Whispers of the Immune

The Doctor's Dilemma Collection, Volume 10

Dr. Nilesh Panchal

Published by DrMedHealth, 2024.

This is a work of fiction. Similarities to real people, places, or events are entirely coincidental.

WHISPERS OF THE IMMUNE

First edition. November 3, 2024.

Copyright © 2024 Dr. Nilesh Panchal.

ISBN: 979-8227439963

Written by Dr. Nilesh Panchal.

Publisher Information

COPYRIGHT © 2024, **DrMedHealth**.

All rights reserved.

No part of this book may be reproduced, distributed, or transmitted in any form or by any means, including photocopying, recording, or other electronic or mechanical methods, without the prior written permission of the publisher, except in the case of brief quotations used for review purposes or academic references.

Under no circumstances will any blame or legal responsibility be held against the publisher, or author, for any damages, reparation, or monetary loss due to the information contained within this book, either directly or indirectly.

Before reading the book, please read the disclaimer.

For permissions, inquiries, or other correspondence:

drmedhealth.com@gmail.com

For more information, please visit.

www.DrMedHealth.com[1]

---

1. http://www.DrMedHealth.com

Disclaimer

THE CONTENT OF THIS book is a work of fiction. Names, characters, places, medical scenarios, and incidents are either the product of the author's imagination or are used fictitiously. Any resemblance to actual persons, living or dead, real-life medical events, organizations, or institutions is purely coincidental.

The medical procedures, treatments, and conditions described are for narrative purposes only and should not be interpreted as professional advice. Readers are advised not to use the medical information presented in this book as a substitute for consulting healthcare professionals or seeking proper medical care.

Neither the author, Dr. Nilesh Panchal, nor the publisher, **DrMedHealth**, assumes any responsibility for actions taken based on the information contained within these novels. Any opinions expressed in the book are solely those of the author and do not represent the views of any affiliated institutions or organizations.

Chapter 1: Patient Zero

The sound of alarms pierced through the sterile corridors of St. Mark's General Hospital, where, until now, the gravest issue had been the flu season's peak. But tonight, something else was brewing, something darker, more insidious. Dr. Mira Kline, an epidemiologist with the CDC, had been called in on an emergency basis. The urgent tone in her director's voice lingered in her mind as she stepped off the elevator on the fourth floor.

The air was thick with antiseptic, mixed with the underlying scent of panic. Nurses were whispering urgently, their eyes flitting around like birds disturbed from a nest. Mira took a deep breath, steadying herself, before making her way to Room 409, where the mystery patient awaited her. The hospital staff called him "Patient Zero."

Mira's supervisor, Dr. Alan Hart, greeted her outside the door. His face was ashen, dark circles bruising the skin under his eyes. He looked like he hadn't slept in days.

"Thank God you're here, Mira," he said, his voice barely above a whisper. "You need to see this for yourself."

Mira's stomach twisted with unease as she followed Dr. Hart inside. She wasn't prepared for what she saw. The man in the bed was barely recognizable as human. His skin was an unnatural shade of gray, mottled with dark, bruise-like patches that spread across his arms and chest. His breathing was ragged, shallow, each inhale seeming like it would be his last.

"How long has he been like this?" Mira asked, her voice steady, though her insides churned.

"Two days," Dr. Hart replied, his gaze fixed on the patient. "He came in with flu-like symptoms: fever, chills, fatigue. But within hours, he deteriorated rapidly. The bruising started about six hours ago. He's been slipping in and out of consciousness since."

Mira frowned, leaning in to inspect the man closer. The dark patches on his skin weren't just bruises; they seemed almost alive, pulsing faintly under the surface. She'd never seen anything like it.

"What's his background?" she asked, pulling up a chair to examine his chart.

"Construction worker. Traveled to a rural area recently, about a hundred miles from here," Dr. Hart said. "No known contacts with anyone else who's shown similar symptoms."

"Yet," Mira murmured, her mind racing. If this was the beginning of something infectious, time was not on their side.

Suddenly, the man convulsed, his body jerking against the restraints the nurses had put in place. Mira jumped back, feeling a surge of adrenaline, her hand instinctively going to her pocket where she kept her phone. In a flash, the man's eyes opened, bloodshot and glassy, as if looking through her rather than at her.

"They're... coming," he whispered, his voice like a crackle of static, barely audible.

"Who's coming?" Mira asked, though she knew he likely wasn't in his right mind.

The man's gaze drifted, unfocused, as his lips parted in a pained exhale. The pulse beneath his skin slowed until, finally, it stopped. A long, ringing silence filled the room. Mira stared at the body, a wave of dread washing over her.

Dr. Hart was the first to break the silence. "We need a sample of his blood, and a full autopsy as soon as possible. If this is infectious—"

"It could already be too late," Mira finished for him. The implications were chilling. If this pathogen could progress from mild symptoms to death in just forty-eight hours, it was unlike anything she'd ever encountered.

As the night stretched on, Mira busied herself with the protocols. She suited up in full protective gear, meticulously swabbing surfaces and collecting samples from the patient's body. But something about the man's condition gnawed at her. It wasn't just a virus, she thought. There was an intelligence to the way it spread, an almost methodical approach as it consumed the body, leaving traces as if marking its territory.

Hours later, exhausted and emotionally drained, Mira returned to her hotel room. She tried to sleep, but her mind replayed the patient's final words. *They're coming.*

The next morning, Mira woke to a barrage of calls and messages. Five new cases had appeared in the city overnight, each exhibiting the same symptoms as Patient Zero. In a small conference room back at the hospital, Mira met with the team she'd assembled to start identifying the pathogen.

"Has anyone seen anything like this?" she asked, as images from the autopsy flickered on the screen.

Dr. Rena Patel, one of the hospital's infectious disease specialists, shook her head. "Nothing like this. The pathogen is aggressive, tearing through cell walls in a way that resembles some of the more deadly hemorrhagic fevers, but it's not presenting in the same way. No bleeding from the eyes or mouth. The bruising is unique."

Mira nodded, her eyes narrowing as she analyzed the data. "It's almost like it's rewriting the body's cellular structure."

"Or hijacking it," Rena suggested.

The implications were terrifying. A pathogen capable of manipulating the body at the cellular level could be a nightmare to contain. They had to determine its mode of transmission, its point of origin, and how it targeted its hosts. But with every minute, the number of cases was rising.

By the end of the day, the count had risen to forty-two. Emergency rooms across the city were overrun, and rumors of an "invisible plague" had begun to spread among the public. Social media lit up with posts, each more frantic than the last, describing symptoms, sharing conspiracy theories, and offering dubious remedies.

Mira knew the panic was only beginning. As she and her team raced against the clock to identify the pathogen, the city's anxiety turned to fear, then anger. People demanded answers, but all Mira could offer was uncertainty.

It was in the early hours of the morning, just as Mira was about to catch a few hours of sleep, that she received an urgent call from Dr. Hart.

"You need to come back to the hospital immediately," he said, his voice tight with tension.

When she arrived, Mira found Dr. Hart and Rena in the lab, their faces pale as they stared at a screen displaying the blood sample from Patient Zero. Mira leaned over, studying the image closely. At first glance, it looked like any other blood sample, but as she examined it closer, she realized what was so unnerving.

The pathogen was still active.

"Is that... even possible?" Mira asked, her voice barely a whisper.

Dr. Hart nodded, his face drawn. "It's not just possible. It's adapting."

The pathogen was behaving in a way that defied everything they understood about infectious diseases. It was as if it had a mind of its own, constantly evolving, seeking new ways to infect its host. And the most terrifying part? There was no way to predict how it would mutate next.

Mira felt a cold sweat break out on her forehead as she processed the implications. If this pathogen could survive outside a host, there would be no containing it. Every surface, every breath, every touch could become a potential vector for infection.

"What about containment?" Rena asked, her voice trembling. "If it's adapting like this, can we even contain it?"

Mira shook her head. "We don't have enough information yet. But if this continues to spread at the current rate... we'll have to consider extreme measures."

"Quarantine?" Dr. Hart asked, though they both knew the city was already past that point. If containment had been possible, they had missed their chance.

As dawn broke, Mira felt a grim determination settle over her. She didn't have the answers yet, but she knew one thing for certain: they were at war. This pathogen wasn't just a virus. It was a predator, and humanity was its prey.

But she refused to be defeated. If there was even a sliver of hope, she would find it. They would study this pathogen, learn its weaknesses, and, if possible, find a way to stop it.

The world had changed overnight, and Mira Kline was on the front lines. She would uncover the truth, no matter the cost.

Chapter 2: Silent Carriers

The quarantine zone outside St. Mark's General had turned into a fortress overnight. Security checkpoints and metal barricades blocked off every entrance and exit, and armored guards stood vigilant, their presence a grim reminder of the invisible threat lurking within the city. For Dr. Mira Kline, the atmosphere of tension was palpable, weighing on her as she strode down the corridor leading to the lab.

Overnight, new cases of the pathogen had flooded the hospital—children, the elderly, and the strong alike were succumbing, each displaying the bruising, the shallow breaths, the haunting final stages Mira had first seen in Patient Zero. The progression was terrifying in its speed and its cruelty.

Yet, in the darkness of the outbreak, a strange phenomenon had caught Mira's attention. A handful of individuals, those in close contact with the infected, remained untouched. Some were spouses, parents, even roommates of the afflicted, and yet they displayed none of the telltale symptoms. Theories churned in Mira's mind—genetics, immune strength, or pure, unexplainable luck?

She was determined to find out.

Mira's first appointment was with Peter Nolan, a firefighter who'd brought in his wife two days prior after she collapsed at their home. As Mira walked into the exam room, Peter looked up with bloodshot eyes and an exhausted expression.

"Dr. Kline?" he asked, his voice a rough whisper. "Any news about Sarah?"

Mira hesitated. Sarah Nolan was one of the more severe cases. Last night, her vitals had plummeted, and despite the team's best efforts, she was in a medically induced coma. Mira knew what he wanted to hear but could only offer honesty.

"She's still critical, Peter. We're doing everything we can," Mira replied gently. "But I need to ask you some questions about your own health."

Peter's brows furrowed in confusion. "My health? I'm fine, Doctor. Just worried sick about Sarah."

"That's exactly it," Mira said. "You've been in close contact with her, more than anyone else, but you're not showing any symptoms."

Peter shrugged, the corners of his mouth pulling down. "Guess I got lucky?"

"That might be the case," Mira replied. "But there might be something else protecting you. We're trying to identify patterns—anything that could help us understand why some people are immune. Would you be willing to answer some questions and go through a few tests?"

"Anything, if it'll help Sarah," Peter said, his eyes reflecting a mixture of hope and desperation. "Ask away."

Mira took a seat, pulling out her tablet. "Tell me everything you can about your health history, any illnesses, medications, allergies."

The session went on for nearly an hour, Mira carefully documenting every detail Peter could remember. His family history, his diet, even his exercise routines—anything that might be a potential lead. He answered patiently, his voice steady, his focus clear despite the chaos outside. Yet, by the end, Mira was left with more questions than answers. There was nothing remarkable about Peter's health. No rare conditions, no unusual resilience. He was simply... unaffected.

Mira concluded the interview with a blood sample, hoping the lab tests would reveal something her questioning hadn't. After collecting samples from several other individuals in similar circumstances, she returned to her lab. Each sample held the potential for discovery, each one a possible window into immunity.

Hours passed as Mira and her team examined the samples. The initial tests showed nothing out of the ordinary—no specific antibodies, no genetic markers that immediately stood out. Yet, Mira had a nagging feeling she was missing something. She knew the answer was there, buried somewhere in the data, waiting to be found.

It was late when Mira's assistant, Jamie, approached her, looking fatigued but excited. "Dr. Kline, I think we found something," he said, handing her a printout.

Mira's eyes scanned the page, her heart quickening. It was subtle, almost invisible to the untrained eye, but Jamie was right. The samples from the immune individuals shared a faint but distinct signature—a genetic variation in one particular sequence that hadn't appeared in any of the infected patients.

"It's... a mutation?" Mira muttered, leaning closer to the printout. "But not a mutation associated with disease. More like an anomaly that disrupts the pathogen's ability to take hold."

Jamie nodded. "That's what it looks like. This sequence—it's blocking something in the pathogen's replication process, almost like it's jamming the signal."

Mira stared at the printout, her mind racing. If this anomaly was the key to immunity, it could mean a breakthrough, a way to contain the outbreak, maybe even a cure. But it was still theoretical, untested.

"This needs to be confirmed," she said, already planning the next steps. "We'll need a larger sample size, more tests. But Jamie... this could be it. We might have found a way forward."

But as she spoke, a flicker of doubt crossed her mind. This mutation was rare, almost one in a million. If immunity depended on this specific anomaly, the chances of finding enough immune individuals were slim. She also had to consider the ethical dilemma this raised. If the mutation was rare, how would the world react to knowing only a select few were safe?

Her thoughts were interrupted by the shrill ring of her phone. It was Dr. Hart, calling from the ICU.

"Mira, you need to get down here," he said, his voice tense. "We've got an incident with one of the immune."

She hurried down the stairs, her mind racing through worst-case scenarios. Was it possible that one of the immune individuals had developed symptoms after all? Had the pathogen mutated, found a way past the genetic defense?

When she arrived in the ICU, Dr. Hart was waiting for her outside a room. Inside, Peter Nolan was lying on a hospital bed, his face pale and his eyes closed.

"What happened?" Mira asked, her voice sharp with urgency.

"He collapsed while visiting his wife," Dr. Hart explained. "He's stable now, but we're seeing some strange results in his bloodwork. It's almost like..."

Mira's stomach twisted as she watched Peter through the glass. "Like he's... changing?"

Dr. Hart nodded. "The genetic signature we detected—it's weakening. It's as if the pathogen has found a way to bypass the immunity."

A chill ran down Mira's spine. If the pathogen could adapt to overcome immunity, then no one was safe—not even those who had shown resistance. Her mind raced, grappling with the implications. They were running out of time, and if the pathogen was adapting at this pace, they needed to act faster.

"What are our options?" she asked, turning to Dr. Hart.

Chapter 3: The Last Safe Haven

The helicopter's blades whipped a fierce wind through the helipad as Dr. Mira Kline stepped forward, her figure small against the towering landscape of mountains and fog. She gripped the edges of her jacket, her mind swimming with unanswered questions. Only a few hours ago, she'd been summoned from the hospital quarantine zone to a secure location known only to select officials. It was clear they were running out of time, and those in power were beginning to pull every string available.

The pilot, a man who'd introduced himself as Commander Ward, didn't say much during the flight, though his grim expression suggested he knew more than he let on. The journey itself took over an hour, taking them far from the city's chaos to a location Mira could only guess was deep in the mountains. As they began their descent, she spotted a sprawling compound below, ringed by high fences and patrolled by guards in military fatigues. This was no ordinary research facility.

"Welcome to Haven," Commander Ward announced as the helicopter touched down, his voice barely audible over the roaring blades. Mira felt a prickle of unease at the name. It seemed ironic, given the circumstances.

She disembarked, blinking against the glare of the landing lights. As she approached, a group of officials stood waiting for her. One stepped forward, a tall man with graying hair and a cold, assessing gaze. He extended his hand.

"Dr. Kline, I'm Colonel Isaac Lawson," he said, his grip firm but his face unreadable. "We've been following your work in the quarantine zone. Impressive, considering the circumstances."

Mira nodded, her mind still reeling from the sudden turn her life had taken. "Thank you. But I'd rather get straight to the point. I need to know why I'm here and what this facility has to do with the pathogen we're dealing with."

Lawson nodded, his expression softening a fraction. "Of course. If you'll follow me, all will be explained." He turned, leading her down a series of hallways lined with security checkpoints. Every door required a key card and a retinal scan to open, the walls lined with cameras tracking every movement. Mira felt like a lab specimen herself, each step deepening her apprehension.

After passing through multiple layers of security, they entered a large, sterile room lined with monitors and medical equipment. Inside, scientists and technicians were hunched over computers, studying data on the pathogen's mutations and behaviors. The room buzzed with an air of urgency, people moving with purpose and intensity.

"We established Haven shortly after the first signs of the pathogen appeared," Lawson explained, his voice low. "Our priority was to create a secure environment where we could study the disease safely, away from the general public. We're on the forefront here, Dr. Kline. This is where we're testing survivors—those who appear to be immune."

Mira looked around, her heart racing. "Testing... survivors? Do they know they're here for experimentation?"

Lawson's gaze flickered, his jaw tightening. "They know they're here for the greater good. Our only hope of stopping this pathogen is to understand why some people are immune. We need to isolate the anomaly in their biology, develop a defense from it. These individuals are humanity's best chance."

He motioned to one of the monitors, where a graph displayed the pathogen's growth rate over time. The curve was steep, with spikes marking each adaptation of the virus. "The pathogen is evolving faster than we anticipated. Every hour counts. We need to get ahead of it, and fast."

Mira felt a shiver as she studied the data. She'd seen the pathogen's progression firsthand, but these numbers told a far darker story. If they couldn't find a way to contain it soon, humanity was facing a complete breakdown.

"So, where do I start?" she asked, determined to suppress the doubts bubbling in her mind.

Lawson gestured toward a glass-walled room on the other side of the lab. Inside were two young men and a woman, seated at a table with monitoring devices attached to their arms. They looked weary, their faces pale and drawn, but otherwise healthy.

"These are some of our most recent arrivals," Lawson said. "They've all shown complete immunity to the pathogen, even after direct exposure. We're running genetic tests, biochemical analysis, anything that might explain why they're different."

Mira felt a pang of empathy as she watched them, their expressions listless and resigned. "Are they being held here against their will?"

Lawson hesitated, a flicker of something unreadable in his eyes. "It's complicated, Dr. Kline. The public's panic has reached dangerous levels. People are desperate, looking for scapegoats, cures, anything to hold onto hope. We can't risk releasing them until we're certain we understand their immunity."

She took a deep breath, nodding. "I understand. But they deserve to know the truth, to have a say in what happens to them. Without that, we're not any better than the pathogen we're fighting."

Lawson's jaw tightened. "We do what we must to ensure the survival of the human race, Dr. Kline. If that means a few sacrifices along the way, then so be it."

Mira's stomach twisted, but she kept her face impassive. She needed access to these patients, and challenging Lawson would get her nowhere. "I'd like to start by reviewing their medical histories, family backgrounds, any genetic data you have."

He nodded, signaling to a nearby technician. "Everything you need will be provided. And one more thing—these individuals aren't the only immune people we've identified. We have another group, kept in a separate wing. They've shown slightly different immunity profiles. We believe they might be carrying a secondary mutation that could be useful."

"Secondary mutation?" Mira asked, intrigued. "Can I see them?"

Lawson hesitated again, his expression shifting to one of caution. "In time. For now, focus on the primary group. Once you're ready, we'll move on to the others."

She sensed he was hiding something, but there was no point pressing the issue now. Instead, she turned to the patients in the glass room. Her mind buzzed with questions, theories forming and dissipating as quickly as they came.

After being outfitted with protective gear, Mira entered the room with the three immune individuals. They looked up as she approached, a mixture of hope and fear in their eyes.

"Hello," she greeted them gently, sitting down at the table across from them. "I'm Dr. Mira Kline, and I'll be working with you to understand your immunity. I know this situation is difficult, but I promise you, I'm here to help."

The woman, who looked to be in her twenties, offered a hesitant smile. "I'm Lucy. And this is Ryan and Marcus," she said, gesturing to the two men beside her. "We've been... waiting for answers. None of us understand why we're here."

Mira's heart ached for them. "I'll do my best to give you answers. But first, I need to know about your experience with the outbreak. How did you come to realize you were immune?"

Ryan, a tall man with dark hair and piercing blue eyes, spoke up. "My fiancée got sick first. She was one of the early cases, but I never felt anything. No fever, no bruising, nothing."

Lucy nodded, her voice trembling slightly. "My brother was infected, too. We were sharing a house, and he collapsed right in front of me. I thought... I thought I was next. But I never got sick."

Mira listened, absorbing every detail. These people had faced unimaginable loss, and yet, something in their bodies had protected them. But why?

"Are any of you aware of any genetic conditions, or family members who've shown similar immunity to other illnesses?" she asked, pulling out a notepad.

They shook their heads, looking at each other with uncertainty. "Not that I know of," Lucy said. "But, to be honest, I never paid much attention to medical stuff before all this."

Mira took down their responses, every detail building a larger picture in her mind. But as the interview continued, an unsettling feeling crept over her. Something was missing. These people were healthy, yes, but there was a quiet desperation in their eyes, a resignation she couldn't ignore.

At the end of the session, Mira stood, smiling reassuringly. "Thank you for sharing this with me. I'll do everything I can to help find answers."

As she left the room, her mind churned with thoughts. The data alone wouldn't be enough; she needed more information about the pathogen's behavior in immune bodies, and perhaps more critically, the psychological toll of immunity. She couldn't shake the feeling that these people were hiding something—something more than fear.

She returned to her lab, diving into the research, her focus unbroken as hours slipped by. Her suspicions about the pathogen's complexity grew with every test result. It was as if the virus adapted specifically to evade the human immune system, a sophistication far beyond any naturally occurring pathogen.

By midnight, Mira's eyes were burning from the strain, but her mind wouldn't let her rest. She was on the verge of something significant, she could feel it.

Just as she was preparing to call it a night, the door to her lab opened. Colonel Lawson stepped in, his expression as grim as ever, but something else lingered in his eyes—urgency mixed with uncertainty.

"We've had a development," he said, his voice low.

Mira glanced at him, instantly alert. "What happened?"

"One of the secondary group members has gone into a seizure," Lawson explained, gesturing for her to follow. "You need to see this."

She hurried after him, her mind racing. If one of the immune individuals was exhibiting symptoms, it could mean one of two things: the pathogen was evolving again, or the secondary mutation was behaving in an unpredictable way.

They navigated the labyrinth of hallways until they reached a section of the facility Mira hadn't yet seen. This area was darker, quieter, and guarded even more heavily. Lawson led her into a secure observation room, where several scientists were monitoring a patient through a two-way mirror. Inside, a young man, no older than twenty, lay strapped to a hospital bed, his body writhing as if in the throes of a nightmare.

Mira took in the scene, feeling a chill down her spine. "What's his story?"

"His name's Ethan," Lawson replied. "He's one of the second group—individuals we suspect carry a secondary mutation, something potentially different from the primary group. He was exposed to the pathogen early on, just like the others, but showed no symptoms."

"And now?"

Lawson's lips thinned. "Now, he's having violent seizures. They started a few hours ago and have been escalating."

Mira frowned, watching the tremors rippling through Ethan's body. The secondary mutation might have been protective at first, but it was clear something had triggered this reaction.

"Do we know if he was exposed to anything unusual in the last 24 hours? Any environmental changes, stressors?" Mira asked, reaching for the medical file a nearby technician handed her.

Lawson crossed his arms. "Nothing out of the ordinary. In fact, he's been under strict surveillance since his arrival. No external contact."

Mira flipped through Ethan's medical history, pausing when she saw a note regarding his initial test results. Unlike the primary group, Ethan's bloodwork had shown erratic levels of specific immune cells—cells that normally responded to foreign agents like viruses, but in his case, had been dormant until now.

"His immune system is... reacting," she muttered, more to herself than anyone else.

Lawson raised an eyebrow. "What do you mean?"

"It's as if something dormant was awakened within him," she said, scrutinizing the data. "This might indicate that the secondary mutation is unstable. Rather than a complete immunity, it could act more like a delay or a buffer, keeping the pathogen at bay until some trigger—environmental or biological—sets it off."

Lawson's jaw clenched. "So, you're saying we could be looking at a time bomb with these secondary cases?"

Mira nodded, a wave of frustration washing over her. They had been so close to finding a potential key to immunity, but if the secondary group wasn't fully immune, their hope was fading fast.

"Get him stabilized," she instructed the nearby doctors. "I need blood samples from him, stat. And I want scans of his brain activity during the seizures."

As Mira left the observation room, she couldn't shake the image of Ethan, his face twisted in pain, his body helpless against whatever had overtaken him. There was something deeply disturbing about the unpredictability of this mutation. If they couldn't isolate the cause, any attempt to replicate immunity might be futile—or worse, dangerous.

Back in the lab, Mira immediately began examining Ethan's new blood samples. She scanned each slide under the microscope, her eyes searching for anything that could explain his sudden reaction. Her mind replayed what she knew of the pathogen, of its ability to adapt and mutate, and of the unpredictable genetic variations in its victims.

Hours passed, and the lab grew quiet as night turned into dawn. Finally, Mira spotted something that made her heart skip. Ethan's cells were undergoing a transformation, but it wasn't viral replication she was seeing. It was something... new.

His white blood cells were forming clusters, almost as if they were attempting to isolate and contain the pathogen on a microscopic level. It was a remarkable sight, unlike any immune response she'd ever witnessed. The cells appeared to be creating a network, a defense mechanism that was simultaneously attacking the pathogen while forming a wall around it.

Mira sat back, her mind racing. If she could isolate this response, it might offer a way to contain the pathogen without requiring a full immune response. It was a narrow thread of hope, but it was hope nonetheless.

Suddenly, her lab phone rang, breaking the silence. She picked it up, her pulse quickening. "Dr. Kline."

"Dr. Kline, this is Jamie. You need to come back to the observation room immediately."

Mira froze. "What happened?"

"It's Ethan... He's—he's lucid," Jamie said, his voice edged with disbelief. "And he's asking for you."

Mira made her way back to the observation room, her heart pounding. When she entered, Ethan was sitting up in bed, his face pale but his eyes sharp. He watched her approach, his gaze intense, as if he'd been waiting for this moment.

"Dr. Kline," he said, his voice steady. "They told me you're the one trying to figure out why I'm... different."

Mira nodded, taking a seat beside his bed. "Yes. I'm trying to understand why some people like you are immune, or at least resistant. You're one of the very few who have this specific secondary mutation, and I believe it's giving you a delayed reaction to the pathogen."

Ethan looked away, his jaw tight. "I never asked for this. I watched my friends die, watched people fall apart, while I just... stayed normal. But I'm not normal, am I?"

"No, Ethan," Mira replied softly. "You're unique. And your immunity could help us save countless lives."

He closed his eyes, a faint smile of bitterness crossing his face. "I'd like to believe that. But this isn't the gift you think it is. I feel it in my body, like a shadow, waiting to take over. That seizure... I thought I was done for."

Mira reached out, placing a reassuring hand on his shoulder. "Whatever this mutation is, it's giving us clues. If we can understand it, we might be able to develop a defense. You're part of something important, something bigger than yourself."

Ethan looked at her, his eyes filled with a desperate kind of hope. "Then don't waste any more time. Whatever you need, just... take it. I don't want anyone else to feel this."

Mira nodded, filled with a renewed determination. She excused herself, instructing the medical team to keep monitoring Ethan closely, and returned to her lab with new urgency. She had a working theory now: the secondary mutation, while unstable, could act as a form of controlled immunity if harnessed correctly.

The hours blurred together as Mira worked, isolating Ethan's cells and attempting to replicate the clustering effect she'd observed. She tested sample after sample, tweaking variables, pushing herself to the brink. The stakes were too high to rest.

Finally, as the first rays of dawn began to stream through the lab's small windows, Mira managed a breakthrough. One of the samples had successfully replicated Ethan's cellular response. She watched in awe as the cells created a self-contained barrier around a weakened form of the pathogen, halting its progression entirely.

It was an extraordinary moment. If she could expand this finding, she might be able to develop a serum—something that could trigger a controlled immune response in uninfected individuals, potentially offering them protection.

But just as the hope began to settle in, a loud banging on the lab door shattered the calm. Mira turned to see Colonel Lawson storming in, his face flushed with anger.

"Dr. Kline, what the hell are you doing?" he demanded.

She straightened, taken aback. "I'm making progress. I think I've found a way to—"

"We don't have time for theories," Lawson snapped. "The pathogen has spread to three new regions, including the capital. The government is implementing martial law. We need results, now."

Mira bristled. "This is as close to a result as anyone's come. If we can synthesize a serum—"

Lawson cut her off, his eyes cold. "You're not here to play scientist, Dr. Kline. You're here to find answers that can be applied immediately. We don't have the luxury of waiting."

She felt a surge of frustration but held her tongue, forcing herself to remain calm. "Colonel, I'm asking for a little more time. We're on the verge of a breakthrough."

Lawson stared at her, his expression hard. For a long moment, he said nothing, and Mira held her breath, waiting for his response.

Finally, he sighed, his shoulders slumping slightly. "Fine. You have forty-eight hours. But if we don't see something concrete by then, we'll be forced to take more drastic measures."

As he turned to leave, Mira felt a pang of dread. She knew what "drastic measures" entailed—quarantine zones, forced isolation, possibly even culling infected areas to prevent further spread.

She couldn't let that happen. Not when she was so close.

Determined, she turned back to her lab equipment, redoubling her efforts. She worked through the day, scarcely noticing the passage of time. With each test, each adjustment, the serum began to take shape, the pieces of the puzzle falling into place.

And finally, after what felt like an eternity, she held a vial of the experimental serum in her hands. It was untested, unproven, but it was the culmination of everything she'd learned from Ethan's mutation.

Her hands trembled slightly as she placed the vial in the refrigerator, her mind a whirlwind of exhaustion and exhilaration. She needed to test it, but that would require a volunteer, someone willing to take the risk.

A familiar face entered her mind: Ethan. He had nothing to lose, and perhaps everything to gain.

But as she prepared to go to him, a new, unbidden thought surfaced, a sliver of doubt she hadn't anticipated.

If this serum worked, it could change the world. But if it failed, if it mutated... it could bring a whole new nightmare.

And in that moment, Mira realized that the stakes were even higher than she'd imagined.

Chapter 4: Code of the Pathogen

Dr. Mira Kline sat in the dim glow of her lab, her eyes scanning the pathogen's genetic sequence projected on the screen before her. The room was silent except for the hum of machinery and the rhythmic ticking of the clock on the wall. She'd been working for hours, running analysis after analysis, delving deeper into the microscopic world of a virus that had already claimed thousands of lives. But this time, she wasn't just looking for answers—she was looking for secrets.

Something had shifted in her understanding of the pathogen. The erratic behavior, the rapid mutations, the relentless speed of its progression—all of it hinted at a mindlessness that had a purpose. She had initially dismissed the idea as paranoia born of stress and sleepless nights, but as she continued her research, patterns began to emerge. Patterns that made her question everything she thought she knew about virology.

She pulled up the pathogen's genetic sequence on the screen, her eyes narrowing as she zoomed in on a particular segment. It was a small string of proteins, easy to overlook if one wasn't looking closely. But Mira had seen enough viruses to recognize when something didn't belong. This was no natural anomaly.

"Jamie," she called, her voice low but urgent. Her assistant looked up from his work at the other end of the lab, a weary expression on his face.

"Yes, Dr. Kline?"

"Come here. I need you to see this."

Jamie walked over, peering at the screen as Mira pointed to the sequence. "See that?"

He squinted, confusion knitting his brow. "It's... unusual, but I'm not sure what it means."

Mira nodded, her heart pounding as she explained. "This sequence isn't random. It's been engineered. Someone altered it deliberately, possibly to enhance the virus's transmissibility or its ability to evade the immune system."

Jamie's face went pale. "Are you saying... this was bioengineered?"

Mira exhaled, struggling to control the storm of emotions building within her. "It's too early to say definitively, but... yes. This sequence doesn't appear in any known viruses. It's as if it was designed specifically to fit like a key in a lock."

She watched Jamie's face as he processed this information, the same horror she felt mirrored in his eyes. This discovery changed everything. If the pathogen was engineered, that meant it wasn't just a freak accident of nature—it was a weapon, and whoever had created it had unleashed it on the world with devastating precision.

Jamie finally spoke, his voice barely above a whisper. "Do we have any leads on where it came from? Any information on possible labs that could have... developed something like this?"

Mira shook her head. "No, not yet. But we need to find out. This sequence—someone out there has the original code, the blueprint. If we can get access to that, we might have a chance at reversing this."

Her mind raced, thinking of all the implications. If the pathogen had indeed been engineered, it might have a failsafe, a hidden vulnerability. Whoever created it would likely have designed a way to control it, or at least minimize its effects on certain populations. But finding that failsafe would be like searching for a needle in a haystack.

"Let's keep this between us for now," she said, glancing at Jamie. "Until we know more, this information could cause a panic. We'll work on isolating this sequence, see if we can learn anything more about its function."

Jamie nodded, his face set in grim determination. "Understood, Dr. Kline. I'll start running a deeper analysis right away."

As Jamie returned to his workstation, Mira turned back to her screen, her mind awash with theories and questions. The thought of a bioengineered pathogen filled her with a combination of dread and anger. It was one thing to battle a natural disease, an evolutionary force of nature. But to think that someone had deliberately unleashed this plague—it was almost too much to bear.

She decided to dig into whatever public databases she could access, searching for information on labs with the capability and resources to create something so deadly. Her fingers flew across the keyboard as she cross-referenced scientific journals, research grants, and government records. Hours passed, the room dimming as the sun dipped below the horizon, but Mira barely noticed. She was on a mission, and she wouldn't stop until she had answers.

Eventually, she stumbled upon a research facility she hadn't considered before: BioSphere International, a high-security lab renowned for its cutting-edge genetic research. Mira's eyes narrowed as she read through the lab's recent projects, many of which focused on virus enhancement for medical research. She knew that in the wrong hands, such research could easily be weaponized.

"BioSphere International," she murmured to herself, making a note of the name. If anyone had the resources and expertise to create a pathogen like this, it would be them.

Mira's phone buzzed, jolting her from her thoughts. It was a message from Dr. Hart, her supervisor back at the quarantine zone. The message was brief, but it sent a chill down her spine: *Need to talk. Urgent. Meet me in my office ASAP.*

Without wasting a moment, Mira grabbed her coat and headed out of the lab, her mind racing with possibilities. She arrived at Dr. Hart's office a short while later, finding him seated behind his desk, his face pale and drawn.

"Dr. Kline," he greeted her, motioning for her to take a seat. "I just received some classified information, and I thought you should know."

"What is it?" she asked, her heart pounding.

Dr. Hart leaned forward, lowering his voice. "I have a contact in the Department of Defense. He reached out to me earlier today, and he confirmed that the government has been aware of the possibility of bioengineered pathogens for years. There have been programs—black-budget projects—where viruses were manipulated for so-called 'defensive' purposes."

Mira's hands clenched in her lap. "And this pathogen... does it have anything to do with those projects?"

Dr. Hart hesitated, then nodded. "My contact couldn't say for sure, but he hinted that something went wrong. There was an 'incident' at a lab a few months back, and certain... materials went missing. It's possible this pathogen was part of those materials."

Mira felt a wave of anger and betrayal wash over her. If the government had been involved in developing such a dangerous virus, and it had now spiraled out of control, the implications were staggering.

"Do you have any leads on where this lab is?" she asked, her voice tight with controlled fury.

Dr. Hart shook his head. "No, but I'm working on it. I've also been told to keep quiet about this. If word gets out, there could be political consequences—potential international fallout."

"Political consequences?" Mira scoffed, unable to hide her frustration. "Thousands of people are dying, and they're worried about politics?"

"I know," Dr. Hart replied, his expression weary. "But that's the world we're in. We have to tread carefully."

Mira took a deep breath, forcing herself to calm down. "I don't care about the politics, Dr. Hart. I care about finding a way to stop this pathogen before it wipes us all out. If BioSphere International or any other lab was involved, we need access to their research. There might be a way to reverse-engineer a solution."

Dr. Hart nodded, looking impressed by her resolve. "I'll see what I can do. But in the meantime, be careful, Mira. You're stepping into dangerous territory. There are people who would do anything to keep this under wraps."

She left his office, her mind buzzing with everything she'd learned. The pieces were beginning to fit together, but the picture they formed was terrifying. Someone, somewhere, had created this virus. And now that it had escaped, the consequences were beyond anything she could have imagined.

Back at her lab, Mira resumed her work with renewed determination. She scrutinized the engineered sequence again, studying its structure, looking for any clue as to how it might be neutralized. She knew the answer was buried in the code—it had to be.

Then, as she delved deeper, she noticed something peculiar. There was a redundancy in the code, a segment that seemed to serve no obvious purpose. It was as if someone had left a backdoor, a way to control or deactivate the pathogen under specific conditions. It was faint, almost invisible, but unmistakable to a trained eye.

Mira's pulse quickened. If this redundancy was intentional, it meant that the pathogen wasn't just a weapon—it was a weapon with a built-in failsafe. Whoever created it had planned for a way to shut it down.

But how?

She examined the sequence, searching for any triggers that might activate the failsafe. It was like trying to solve a puzzle with half the pieces missing, but Mira refused to give up. She knew she was onto something, something that could change the course of the outbreak.

Finally, after hours of meticulous analysis, she found it. The pathogen's failsafe was linked to a specific environmental trigger—a protein that only appeared in certain populations, a subtle marker that would render the virus inert in those who carried it. But this protein was rare, appearing in less than one percent of the population.

The realization hit her like a punch to the gut. The failsafe wasn't meant to save humanity. It was meant to save a select few, those who carried the specific genetic marker. This pathogen wasn't just a random bioweapon—it was a targeted tool, designed to wipe out vast swathes of the population while sparing a chosen few.

Mira's mind raced with the implications. This was beyond unethical, beyond monstrous. Whoever had created this virus had intended to control who lived and who died, to reshape society on a genetic level.

Her first impulse was to expose everything, to shout the truth from the rooftops. But she knew that wouldn't help. The pathogen was already out there, ravaging the world. What mattered now was finding a way to disable it, to activate the failsafe on a global scale.

She began working frantically, experimenting with ways to synthesize the trigger protein. If she could create a version that could be distributed widely, it might activate the failsafe in enough people to halt the spread of the virus.

But the process was complex, and time was against her. The pathogen continued to spread, claiming lives by the thousands. Mira's only hope was that she could stay ahead of it, that she could find a way to use the failsafe before it was too late.

As the hours passed, Mira felt her resolve harden. She was no longer just a scientist—she was a soldier in a war against an invisible enemy, a war that had already claimed too many lives.

Finally, as dawn broke, she held a vial of the synthesized protein in her hands. It was untested, unproven, but it was all she had. She knew the risks, knew that this protein might do nothing, or worse, trigger an even deadlier mutation. But she had no choice.

She injected a sample of the pathogen into a test subject—one of the few infected animals they had on-site, a small rabbit whose breathing was labored from the virus. Carefully, she administered the protein, watching anxiously as she monitored the animal's vitals.

For a long moment, nothing happened. Then, slowly, the rabbit's breathing began to stabilize. Its heartbeat, which had been erratic, settled into a steady rhythm. Mira felt a surge of hope. The protein was working.

She repeated the test on several other infected animals, each one showing the same response. It was a small victory, but it was a victory nonetheless. She'd found a way to activate the failsafe, to shut down the pathogen's lethal effects.

But as she prepared to scale up her efforts, the lab door swung open, and Colonel Lawson entered, his face unreadable.

"What are you doing, Dr. Kline?" he asked, his voice cold.

Mira hesitated, holding up the vial of protein. "I've found a way to trigger the failsafe. This could save lives, Colonel. We need to start distribution immediately."

Lawson's eyes narrowed, and Mira sensed a tension in the air, a darkness she hadn't noticed before.

"You weren't authorized to work on this," he said quietly. "You've gone too far."

Mira stared at him, a sinking feeling in her stomach. "What do you mean? This is our only chance to stop the pathogen. We can't afford to waste time."

Lawson shook his head. "This isn't your decision to make, Dr. Kline. You're dealing with forces you don't understand."

He stepped forward, reaching for the vial in her hand. Mira tightened her grip, refusing to let go. She felt a surge of defiance, a fierce determination to protect what she had discovered.

"I won't let you take this," she said, her voice steady. "People are dying, Colonel. I can't just stand by and do nothing."

Lawson's gaze hardened, a dangerous glint in his eyes. "You're playing with fire, Dr. Kline. And if you don't hand over that vial, you may end up burned."

Mira's heart pounded, but she stood her ground, her resolve unshakable.

This was a battle she was willing to fight, no matter the cost.

Chapter 5: Into the Red Zone

The whir of the helicopter blades echoed in Dr. Mira Kline's ears as she stared down through the glass to the ground below. The city spread out beneath her like a war zone, once-busy streets now eerily quiet, buildings abandoned, windows shattered. The Red Zone, as it was now called, spanned miles, containing the highest concentration of pathogen cases and the worst of its devastation. This was the heart of the outbreak, the place where the infection had taken its deepest roots, leaving an undeniable scar across the landscape.

Only a few weeks ago, this area had been bustling with life—shops, schools, people hurrying along with their daily routines. Now, those routines were shattered. The pathogen had moved through the population with a relentless, insatiable hunger, taking thousands in a matter of days. And now, the city stood as a testament to its fury, a silent, decaying monument to the invisible enemy they were all fighting.

"You sure about this, Dr. Kline?" The voice of Lieutenant Jake Turner, the soldier accompanying her, cut through her thoughts. He was seated across from her, his hands gripping the handle of his gun tightly, his eyes watching her with a mixture of respect and concern.

She nodded, her jaw set in determination. "We need answers, and the only way to get them is to see this up close."

Turner looked at her for a moment before nodding, as if resigning himself to her resolve. "Just remember, we get in, do what we need to do, and get out. I'm under strict orders not to let anything happen to you, Doctor."

Mira offered a slight smile. "I appreciate the concern, Lieutenant, but I'm here to do my job. If we don't get the data we need, this thing won't stop spreading. We'll be risking more than just our lives."

The helicopter began its descent, and Mira braced herself as they touched down in the makeshift landing zone. Outside, a group of soldiers in biohazard suits awaited them, armed and tense, their eyes scanning the empty streets. As she stepped out, Mira took a deep breath, the sterile smell of her suit filtering through the respirator. Despite the layers of protection, a chill ran through her spine as she surveyed the city. Every surface, every breath of air was potentially contaminated.

She followed Lieutenant Turner and the team through the deserted streets, the eerie silence pressing down on them like a physical weight. There were no birds, no rustling leaves—only the sound of their footsteps and the occasional murmur of their respirators.

"Dr. Kline," Turner said, his voice muffled through his suit. "We're heading to Ground Zero first, the apartment complex where the initial cases were identified. It's the most concentrated area of infection, but it should give you the best chance to see the pathogen's effects firsthand."

Mira nodded, her heart pounding. The apartment complex was a fifteen-story building on the outskirts of downtown. The pathogen had ravaged its inhabitants with brutal efficiency, and reports suggested that those who hadn't fled had died within days of infection. This place was now abandoned, a hotbed of the virus that had spread outward like ripples from a stone dropped in a pond.

As they approached the building, Mira felt the weight of what she was about to witness. She had studied pandemics, read about historical outbreaks, but nothing had prepared her for this. The building loomed over them, its windows dark, a few broken and open to the elements. It looked like a monument of death, a place where life had been snuffed out in every room, every hallway.

"Let's move," Turner said, his voice tense. "Stay close, and don't touch anything unless absolutely necessary."

They entered the lobby, the air stale and thick. Mira could feel the presence of those who had once lived here, their lives abruptly interrupted. They passed through the main corridor, which led to the elevators, though these had long stopped working. Instead, they took the stairs, their footsteps echoing in the narrow shaft as they climbed, floor by floor.

The first few levels were mostly deserted, a scattering of abandoned furniture and personal belongings littering the halls. But as they reached the upper floors, Mira noticed signs of the pathogen's work: dried blood smeared on walls, clothing left behind in haste, and, occasionally, the remnants of bodies, now reduced to skeletal remains draped in the tattered remnants of their clothes.

On the tenth floor, Turner paused, his hand raised to signal a stop. "This is where the highest concentration of cases were reported," he said. "We've set up a lab station in one of the rooms."

They entered a small, dimly lit apartment, where a makeshift laboratory had been arranged. Testing equipment sat on a rickety table next to the window, and samples of various materials from the building lay in carefully labeled containers. Mira took a deep breath, steadying herself. This was why she'd come—to collect data, to find answers, and to confront the pathogen in its purest form.

She approached the testing equipment, methodically checking each piece to ensure everything was in working order. Then, she moved to the samples, her gloved hands reaching for a petri dish containing a swab from one of the surfaces outside.

"This is where it all began," she murmured to herself, as she examined the specimen under the portable microscope. The pathogen was visible even in this crude setting, a web of microscopic particles clustered together, pulsating with an eerie vitality. It was astonishingly aggressive, its cells seeming to vibrate with energy, as if actively seeking a new host.

"Unbelievable," she whispered. "It's like it's... alive."

Lieutenant Turner, watching over her shoulder, shifted uneasily. "What do you mean?"

Mira looked up, her eyes alight with both fascination and horror. "This isn't like any virus I've seen. It's not just reproducing—it's behaving almost intelligently. It's as if it's actively trying to spread, adapting to its environment in real-time. It's no wonder it's spreading so quickly."

Turner's face hardened. "So, what are we dealing with here, Doctor? A virus with a mind of its own?"

"Not quite," Mira replied, though she was beginning to question even that. "But it's incredibly advanced. It seems capable of surviving on surfaces far longer than any virus we've encountered. And it appears to evolve rapidly, adapting to whatever it encounters, whether that's human cells or environmental changes."

She gathered her samples, each one a piece of the puzzle she was trying to solve. Her mind raced with possibilities, each more terrifying than the last. She knew she had to understand the pathogen's mechanisms before they could hope to contain it, but the task was daunting.

"Let's keep moving," Turner said, glancing around nervously. "This place gives me the creeps."

They continued to the top floors, where the pathogen had taken its heaviest toll. The higher they went, the more signs of death and decay they encountered. Mira's heart ached at the sight of abandoned belongings, family photos, and children's toys, each a reminder of the lives cut short by the virus.

Finally, they reached the penthouse, the supposed origin point of the outbreak. The air was heavy with the scent of decay, and Mira's respirator felt almost useless against the permeating stench. She could barely imagine the horror of those first days, as the virus spread unchecked, its victims isolated and helpless.

In the living room, a table was covered with medical files, research notes, and scattered equipment. Mira's eyes fell on a folder labeled "Experiment Notes." She opened it, her pulse quickening as she scanned the contents. The notes detailed a series of trials involving viral enhancements—experiments with gene splicing, attempts to make the virus more adaptable, more resilient.

"What... is this?" she whispered, her voice trembling. The implications were staggering.

Lieutenant Turner moved closer, his brow furrowing as he looked over her shoulder. "Doctor, are you saying this was... created here?"

Mira swallowed hard, her mind reeling. The research was clear: this wasn't a natural pathogen. It was a weapon, carefully designed and meticulously engineered. Each note detailed the virus's enhancements, each alteration made to increase its efficiency, its lethality.

She closed the folder, her heart racing. "This wasn't just an outbreak, Lieutenant. It was a test. Someone created this virus, and they used this building, these people, as their guinea pigs."

Turner's face went pale. "You're saying they released it... on purpose?"

Mira nodded, her hands trembling. "It looks that way. Whoever did this wanted to see how the virus would spread, how quickly it would adapt. And they chose this building, these people, to watch it happen."

A silence fell over them as the gravity of the revelation settled in. Mira felt a wave of anger, a deep, visceral rage at the thought of innocent lives sacrificed for such a monstrous experiment. She had seen the toll of natural diseases, understood the brutality of nature, but this... this was something else. This was human cruelty at its worst, a calculated act of destruction.

"We have to get out of here," Turner said, his voice barely a whisper. "And we need to report this. People need to know."

Mira nodded, gathering the folder and stuffing it into her pack. She felt a fierce determination settle over her. This information needed to reach the outside world, no matter the cost. She was no longer just a scientist studying a virus—she was a witness to a crime, and she had a duty to expose the truth.

As they made their way back down the stairs, Mira's mind raced with thoughts of how she would report her findings, who she could trust with the information. She knew this would shake the world to its core, the revelation that the virus had been deliberately unleashed, that it was no accident but an act of calculated terror.

They reached the ground floor, and Mira took one last look at the building, feeling a surge of sadness for the lives lost here, the families torn apart. But she couldn't dwell on it now. She had a mission, a purpose, and she wouldn't stop until the truth was known.

The return to the helicopter was tense, the soldiers silent as they absorbed the enormity of what they had just uncovered. As they lifted off, Mira looked down at the city, a grim determination hardening her resolve.

This was just the beginning.

The helicopter ascended, lifting Mira and the soldiers above the silent city, but her mind was firmly grounded in the revelations of the Red Zone. Her heart hammered as she clutched the folder in her lap, her fingers digging into the edges. She couldn't shake the images of the empty apartment complex, the abandoned toys and photos, the signs of lives brutally interrupted. Yet, within her anger and sorrow, there simmered a fierce determination—a commitment to bring justice to the thousands who had suffered.

Lieutenant Turner sat beside her, his face etched with a deep scowl. He kept his eyes on the ground below as the helicopter rose, perhaps unable to look Mira in the eye after witnessing the horrifying truth of the pathogen's origins. They had both been thrust into a realm where morality clashed with duty, and the shock of it weighed heavily on them.

As the helicopter leveled off, Mira turned to Turner. "We have to tell people. This can't stay hidden. If this is what I think it is, then the pathogen has a purpose beyond the outbreak—a far darker one."

Turner's jaw tightened. "I agree. But you know as well as I do that going public won't be easy. The people behind this, whoever they are... they have power. They wouldn't have risked releasing this thing unless they had ways to cover their tracks."

Mira nodded, acknowledging the weight of his words. She knew that whistleblowers rarely emerged unscathed, especially when the stakes were this high. This wasn't just an illegal experiment; it was a crime against humanity, orchestrated and funded by forces capable of unleashing an apocalypse on an unsuspecting world. But if there was one thing Mira knew for certain, it was that her conscience would never allow her to walk away from this.

"Then we'll find a way," she said firmly. "Whatever it takes. We need to examine this data thoroughly. We'll need evidence that can't be buried or denied. Something that shows not only how this pathogen was engineered but who did it and why."

Turner sighed, shaking his head. "It won't be easy, but I'm with you, Doctor. People need to know what's happening here."

They rode the rest of the way in silence, the enormity of their task pressing down on them. As they neared the military compound, Mira's thoughts shifted to the challenges that lay ahead. The scientific community, the government, even her own colleagues—all would be shocked, and some would likely resist believing that such a tragedy had been purposefully set in motion.

As they touched down and the helicopter doors opened, Mira moved quickly toward her lab, the precious folder clutched tightly to her chest. The soldiers peeled off, but Turner followed close behind her, his silence a quiet vow of solidarity. Once they were inside the lab, away from prying eyes, Mira spread the contents of the folder across a table, staring at the scattered notes, diagrams, and photographs.

"It's all here," she muttered, piecing together the evidence in her mind. "They were experimenting with genetic mutations, altering the virus to increase its lethality and its adaptability. These people—they weren't just testing a new drug or vaccine. They were crafting a weapon."

Turner ran a hand through his hair, his face contorted with disgust. "But why? Who gains from something like this?"

Mira shook her head. "There could be any number of reasons. Control, profit, power... Some people view human lives as numbers on a ledger, obstacles in the way of their objectives."

She traced her fingers over the notes, searching for anything that might identify the masterminds behind this scheme. That's when she noticed a faint watermark on one of the pages, partially obscured by handwritten annotations. She adjusted the light, tilting the paper to make out the words.

It read: **BioSphere International—Project Helix.**

Mira's breath caught. BioSphere International—she had suspected them before but hadn't had concrete proof. Now, it was in her hands. Her pulse quickened as she scanned the rest of the notes, uncovering names of research scientists, the funding entities, and logistical details for Project Helix. The project's ultimate goal, though not explicitly stated, was clear from the pathogen's very existence: a viral weapon that could selectively target populations.

"This... this is it," Mira whispered, barely able to contain her shock. "BioSphere International developed this pathogen. Project Helix was their codename for it. They planned this, and they released it here as a test."

Turner's face twisted in horror as he absorbed her words. "They're using it to test population control methods... for warfare."

Mira clenched her fists. "We need to bring this to someone who can make it public—an independent investigator, or even the press."

Turner looked conflicted, the tension clear in his expression. "Dr. Kline, I'm all for getting this out there, but if BioSphere has the power to do this, they'll have allies in high places. We'll need airtight proof, or else they'll bury this faster than we can get the word out."

"Then let's make sure they can't hide it," Mira replied, her resolve hardening. "If we can collect more evidence, get a copy of their records and communications about Project Helix, we'll have an undeniable case."

Turner thought for a moment, then nodded, determination replacing the fear in his eyes. "I know someone in intelligence—someone who might be able to help. But it's a risk. If they're compromised, this could all go very wrong."

"It's a risk we have to take," Mira said, her gaze unwavering. "We owe it to the people who died, and to everyone still at risk."

Over the next several days, Mira and Turner worked tirelessly, gathering every piece of data, cross-referencing information, and searching for connections between BioSphere and the government agencies that might have sanctioned Project Helix. It was exhausting, dangerous work, and both of them lived in constant fear of being discovered. They worked in secret, sometimes in the dead of night, to ensure no one would find out what they were up to.

As their investigation progressed, Mira found herself haunted by nightmares of the Red Zone, of the empty hallways and decaying remains, the life that had been stolen from the people who once lived there. But each time she woke, she returned to her work with renewed resolve. She would honor those lives by revealing the truth.

One evening, as Mira sat reviewing her notes, her phone buzzed. It was a message from Turner, who had gone out to meet his intelligence contact.

We have a problem. Meet me in the basement lab, now.

A chill ran down her spine. She closed her files, tucking them into her bag, and quickly made her way to the lab. When she arrived, she found Turner pacing, his face a mask of anxiety.

"What happened?" Mira asked, closing the door behind her.

Turner took a deep breath. "My contact... he's gone silent. He was supposed to meet me, but when I got to the rendezvous, he wasn't there. I tried calling him, but his line's been disconnected. I think he's been compromised."

Mira's stomach dropped. "That means they know. BioSphere, or someone within the government, knows we're getting close."

Turner nodded, his face grim. "We have to assume they're aware of what we're doing. They might already be looking for us."

Mira's mind raced, her heart pounding as the reality of their situation sank in. They were running out of time, and their options were quickly dwindling. If BioSphere knew they were onto Project Helix, they would stop at nothing to protect their secrets. And that meant Mira and Turner were now targets.

"We need to go public, now," Mira said, her voice resolute. "We have enough evidence to show that BioSphere created this pathogen. We'll take it to the press, to independent scientists—anyone who will listen."

Turner hesitated, but after a moment, he nodded. "Let's do it. But we'll need to be careful. If they're onto us, they'll try to intercept us before we can get the word out."

Together, they devised a plan. They would split up, each taking half of the evidence and contacting separate journalists. They knew it would be risky—if one of them was caught, the other might still succeed. It was a last-ditch effort, a desperate gamble, but it was all they had.

Mira's hands trembled as she packed up her share of the documents, double-checking that everything was accounted for. She had spent her life studying viruses, working tirelessly to understand the mysteries of disease, but this was something else entirely. She was no longer just a scientist. She was a whistleblower, fighting to expose a conspiracy that had claimed thousands of lives.

As she and Turner made their way out of the lab and into the night, Mira felt a strange sense of calm settle over her. She knew the risks, understood that her life was in danger, but she also knew that she was doing the right thing. For the first time since the outbreak began, she felt a glimmer of hope.

"Good luck, Dr. Kline," Turner said, giving her a final nod.

"Stay safe, Lieutenant," she replied, offering him a small, determined smile.

They parted ways, each heading in a different direction, carrying the truth with them like a fragile ember that could ignite a fire. Mira moved through the shadows, her bag clutched tightly to her chest, her heart pounding with a mixture of fear and anticipation.

As she made her way toward her destination, she couldn't shake the feeling that she was being watched. She quickened her pace, glancing over her shoulder, but the streets were empty, the city silent.

She was close now, just a few blocks away from the office of the journalist she had arranged to meet. But as she rounded a corner, she heard footsteps behind her, heavy and purposeful. Panic surged through her as she realized she was being followed.

She broke into a run, her breath coming in ragged gasps as she sprinted down the street. She could hear the footsteps gaining on her, the sound echoing through the empty city.

Finally, she reached the entrance to the building, throwing open the door and dashing inside. She raced up the stairs, her heart pounding, praying she would make it in time.

When she reached the designated floor, she found the journalist waiting, a look of surprise on his face as she burst into the room.

"Dr. Kline?" he asked, his eyes wide.

"Take this," she said, thrusting the folder into his hands. "It's everything—Project Helix, the pathogen, BioSphere International. You have to publish it, get it out to the world."

The journalist nodded, glancing through the documents, his face paling as he realized the magnitude of what he was holding.

But before he could speak, a loud bang echoed through the room, the door flying open as a group of armed men stormed in.

Mira felt a surge of terror as they closed in, their faces hidden behind masks, their weapons trained on her.

"Dr. Kline," one of them said, his voice cold. "You're coming with us."

She looked at the journalist, her eyes pleading. "Please. Don't let them bury this."

He gave a small nod, his hands clutching the folder tightly, his face set with determination.

As the men took her away, Mira felt a strange sense of peace. She had done her part, passed on the torch. The truth was out there now, in the hands of someone who could make a difference.

And no matter what happened next, she knew she had fought for what was right.

Chapter 6: Echoes of Humanity

The light was weak as dawn broke over the desolate landscape. Dr. Mira Kline's cell, located deep within a hidden facility, was cold and unyielding, a stark contrast to the haunting images her mind replayed over and over. The silence felt like a physical presence, pressing down on her, amplifying her thoughts as she processed the devastation that had spread beyond anything she had imagined. All around the world, countries were crumbling, communities lay in ruins, and cities that once stood as symbols of human achievement had become wastelands under the weight of the pathogen's merciless onslaught.

Confined to her cell, Mira spent hours in a state somewhere between sleep and wakefulness, wrestling with memories, questions, and the relentless ache of guilt. She remembered every face she'd seen in the Red Zone, every whisper of life extinguished before its time. With the walls of her cell as her only company, she felt as if she could hear the faint echoes of those lives—their laughter, fears, hopes—all stifled by the virus that had left humanity on the edge of annihilation.

Mira's thoughts drifted to the beginnings of this crisis, to the gradual unraveling of society that had followed the outbreak's spread. It was as if a mirror had been held up to humanity, forcing them to confront their own fragility. Nations had scrambled to protect their borders, citizens turned on one another in a desperate fight for resources, and governments proved powerless against a virus that tore through their populations without regard for wealth, status, or power.

In her mind, she saw news reports from the early days of the outbreak—footage of crowded hospitals, desperate families separated by quarantine lines, riots breaking out as supplies dwindled. All these images merged into a singular, horrific vision of humanity's greatest strengths and weaknesses laid bare. The pathogen hadn't just attacked their bodies; it had exposed the deep-seated flaws that lurked beneath the surface of their civilization. She wondered, in those quiet, private moments, if the world would ever be the same again, and if humanity even deserved another chance.

The thought was painful, but it persisted: had they brought this upon themselves? The experiments, the greed, the relentless pursuit of control over nature without considering the consequences—it was as if humanity had carved its own path to ruin. But even in her bitterness, Mira couldn't ignore the flashes of selflessness she had seen, the acts of bravery in the face of despair. She had seen doctors working tirelessly, risking their lives, and she had watched as friends and family supported one another through unimaginable loss.

One morning, Mira was jolted from her thoughts by the sound of footsteps echoing down the corridor. She sat up, her pulse quickening as the heavy door swung open. Colonel Isaac

Lawson entered, his expression as stoic as ever. He regarded her in silence for a moment before speaking.

"Dr. Kline," he began, his voice even, though Mira could detect a hint of weariness in his eyes. "We need to talk."

Mira forced herself to meet his gaze, unwilling to show any sign of weakness. "I've said everything I had to say, Colonel. The evidence is out there. I'm done hiding the truth."

Lawson's mouth twisted slightly, as if he were amused. "Yes, your... unfortunate incident with the journalist." He sighed, folding his arms. "Do you know what chaos you've unleashed?"

Mira's heart pounded, but she kept her voice steady. "Chaos? I didn't create this pathogen, Colonel. That chaos was already brewing. I just made sure the world knew about it."

Lawson's gaze hardened. "And in doing so, you've accelerated the collapse of everything we've built. Governments are in turmoil, the stock markets have crashed, entire infrastructures are failing. People are dying—not just from the virus, but from panic, starvation, violence. The world is unraveling, and your actions have thrown gasoline on the fire."

Mira's face remained impassive, though her heart ached at his words. "So, you think ignorance would have saved them? That letting people die without understanding what was happening would somehow be better?"

Lawson shook his head. "I think there are times when the truth does more harm than good. When order is all that stands between civilization and chaos."

She felt anger rise in her chest. "Order? You call this order? Thousands are dead, and more will die unless we find a solution. The truth is the only thing that gives people a fighting chance."

Lawson studied her, his expression unreadable. "I didn't come here to debate philosophy with you, Dr. Kline. I came here to offer you a chance to help. You're a brilliant scientist, one of the best we have. We still need answers—answers only you can provide."

Mira scoffed, crossing her arms over her chest. "You want me to go back to work for you? After everything you've done?"

Lawson's gaze didn't waver. "We're beyond morality here, Dr. Kline. The world needs a cure, and you are one of the few people capable of finding it. Put aside your anger and think about the bigger picture. What's more important: proving a point, or saving lives?"

Mira fell silent, the weight of his words settling over her. She despised Lawson and everything he represented, but she couldn't ignore the truth in his statement. She had dedicated her life to studying viruses, to understanding how to protect people from them. She had entered this field not to judge humanity's flaws, but to give them a chance to survive.

With a heavy sigh, she finally nodded. "Fine. I'll help. But on one condition: I work independently. No interference, no lies. If I do this, I do it my way."

Lawson's eyes narrowed, but after a moment, he inclined his head. "Agreed. You'll have access to the lab, and all the resources you need. But understand this: time is running out. You'll need to work fast."

As he left, Mira felt a surge of determination mixed with resignation. She had little trust left in the systems that had betrayed humanity, but she still had faith in science—in the pursuit of answers, in the hope that knowledge could bring about a better future. Even if it meant working within the confines of this twisted organization, she would continue her work. Humanity's flaws might have brought them to this point, but perhaps, just perhaps, their resilience and will to survive could lead them out of it.

Days bled into weeks as Mira threw herself into her research, working around the clock with a singular focus. She studied the pathogen relentlessly, pushing her body and mind to their limits as she searched for a breakthrough. The more she learned, the more she realized just how cunning and adaptive the virus was. Every time she thought she had found a potential solution, the virus would reveal another layer, another mechanism that rendered her efforts useless.

It was during one of these long nights, as she pored over a new set of samples, that Mira's thoughts drifted to the broader implications of her work. The pathogen, in its terrifying efficiency, was a mirror of humanity itself. It consumed, adapted, evolved—just as humans had done for centuries. It spread without regard for borders or social hierarchies, indiscriminately targeting everyone in its path. In a way, it was the ultimate equalizer, forcing people to confront the fragility of life, the impermanence of their accomplishments.

But there was another, deeper truth that haunted her. If humanity survived this, what kind of world would they rebuild? Would they learn from this experience, or would they simply return to the same patterns that had led them to this brink? Mira didn't have the answer, but she knew that survival alone wasn't enough. They needed to understand, to remember, to carry forward the lessons learned in the face of catastrophe.

She thought of the doctors, nurses, and essential workers who had risked their lives to care for others, even as the virus ravaged their communities. She thought of the scientists, like herself, who had dedicated their lives to uncovering knowledge that might one day save humanity from such a fate. And she thought of the everyday people—mothers, fathers, friends—who had endured unimaginable loss, yet continued to persevere.

This was the legacy worth fighting for. Not the power structures or the wealth that had proven so fragile, but the resilience, compassion, and strength that defined humanity at its core. She realized then that her fight wasn't just about finding a cure. It was about preserving the essence of what it meant to be human.

With a renewed sense of purpose, Mira returned to her work, driven by a commitment not just to survival, but to something greater—a legacy of hope, resilience, and humanity.

One evening, as she was deep into another round of tests, she received an unexpected visit. Lawson entered her lab, his usually steely expression softened by something Mira hadn't seen before—doubt.

"Dr. Kline," he said, his voice low. "I... I came to apologize."

Mira looked up, surprised. She had never expected an apology from the man who had been complicit in the world's suffering.

Lawson continued, his gaze distant. "This pathogen, this... disaster. I thought we could control it, that it would be a tool to strengthen our defenses, maybe even unite people against a common enemy. But I see now that we were wrong. This virus has shown us our own darkness, our own arrogance."

Mira studied him, searching for any trace of insincerity, but found none. For the first time, she saw him as more than just a soldier, more than a cog in a ruthless machine. He was a man who, like her, had been forced to confront the consequences of humanity's hubris.

"We all make mistakes, Colonel," she said quietly. "But what matters is what we do to make it right."

Lawson nodded, a flicker of hope in his eyes. "If there's anything I can do to help, anything at all, just say the word."

She gave a small nod, a silent acknowledgment of the fragile alliance they had formed. They were on the same side now—not as adversaries, but as people striving to right a monumental wrong.

With renewed vigor, Mira continued her research, finally reaching a breakthrough in the pathogen's complex genetic structure. She discovered a weak point, a vulnerability buried deep within its code, one that could potentially halt its replication process. It was a small victory, but it was enough to give her hope.

She worked tirelessly, synthesizing a potential treatment, testing it on samples in the lab, and refining it with each iteration. After countless trials, she finally had a prototype—a serum that, if successful, could neutralize the pathogen within an infected host.

The night she completed the serum, Mira felt a profound sense of accomplishment tempered by the knowledge of what lay ahead. She knew that distributing the serum would be a Herculean task, that there would be resistance, setbacks, and sacrifices. But for the first time in weeks, she allowed herself to feel hope.

Hope that the echoes of humanity—the resilience, the compassion, the courage—would outlast the virus. Hope that they would rebuild, not just their cities and societies, but their collective spirit.

As she prepared to begin the first human trials, Mira glanced out the small window of her lab, watching as the first light of dawn crept over the horizon. In that quiet moment, she allowed herself a single, simple thought.

Maybe, just maybe, humanity would endure.

Chapter 7: Genetic Goldmine

Dr. Mira Kline stared at the screen in front of her, a growing sense of awe mingling with unease as she examined the data that pulsed across the monitor. This was the breakthrough she had been searching for, yet it was more than she had bargained for. The unique genetic markers she had identified within the immune population weren't just anomalies—they were the potential key to immunity. But in the wrong hands, they could also be the key to unimaginable destruction.

The work to reach this moment had been grueling, days bleeding into nights, each experiment building on the last. Mira had worked tirelessly, extracting samples, running tests, and analyzing every variable she could think of to pinpoint what made the immune different. Their bodies, it seemed, were equipped with genetic defenses that neutralized the pathogen at its earliest stages, preventing it from ever gaining a foothold. But understanding this mechanism had required her to journey into the heart of genetics, where the smallest variations in DNA sequences could mean the difference between life and death.

Across the lab, her assistant, Jamie, was poring over his own set of data, his brow furrowed in concentration. He looked up as Mira let out a breath she hadn't realized she'd been holding.

"Anything?" he asked, his tone both hopeful and exhausted.

Mira nodded slowly, her gaze fixed on the screen. "More than anything. Look at this." She pointed to a highlighted sequence in the genome. "See these variations? They aren't present in the general population. This group—the immune—they share a unique genetic marker. It's subtle, almost invisible, but it's there. And it seems to be acting as a natural defense."

Jamie leaned in, his eyes widening as he took in the implications. "You're saying... it's like they have a built-in shield?"

"Exactly," Mira replied, excitement edging into her voice. "This marker seems to trigger an immune response that neutralizes the pathogen at a cellular level. It's fast, effective, and—" she hesitated, the gravity of her discovery settling over her, "it's incredibly rare."

Jamie exhaled, shaking his head. "So we're looking at a one-in-a-million genetic lottery? How are we supposed to replicate that?"

"That's the challenge," Mira said, her voice more contemplative. "But if we could isolate this sequence, find a way to mimic its effects..." She didn't need to finish the sentence. The potential was staggering: an immunity serum, a vaccine, perhaps even a cure. But lurking beneath this potential was a darker reality. This genetic marker wasn't just a cure waiting to be unlocked. It was also a blueprint for control.

She turned to Jamie, a new resolve in her gaze. "We need to tread carefully with this information. If it falls into the wrong hands..."

Jamie nodded, understanding her unspoken warning. The power to protect was also the power to destroy, and Mira knew all too well how easily science could be twisted to serve darker agendas. She had uncovered the first pieces of a genetic weapon, one that could be wielded with precision if manipulated by those seeking control.

As they worked, her mind drifted back to a conversation she'd had with Colonel Lawson days earlier. He had called her discovery of a potential serum a "game-changer," but she had sensed the glint in his eyes—the hunger for a weapon rather than a cure. She shuddered to think what people like him would do with the ability to manipulate immunity at will.

She knew she couldn't keep her findings a secret forever. But before she revealed anything, she needed to understand it fully. Over the following days, Mira and Jamie threw themselves into their work, running simulation after simulation, testing every possible variable to verify their findings. It was exhausting, relentless work, but the closer they got, the more Mira's anxiety grew. She was no longer just looking at data; she was unraveling a delicate web of genetic code that held humanity's fate within it.

One evening, as Mira sat alone in the lab reviewing the latest results, the quiet was broken by the sound of the door sliding open. She looked up to see Colonel Lawson, his face a mask of barely restrained impatience.

"Dr. Kline," he began, striding across the lab with the authority of a man who was used to getting what he wanted. "I understand you've made progress. I'd like to hear about it."

Mira hesitated, her mind racing through her options. She knew that revealing too much would put her work—and possibly countless lives—at risk. But she also knew that stalling might arouse suspicion.

"We've identified a potential marker," she said carefully. "It's rare, but it appears to grant immunity by triggering a hyper-efficient immune response. We're still analyzing the specifics, but it's a promising lead."

Lawson's eyes gleamed, and Mira felt a pang of unease. "And this marker—is it something we could extract? Perhaps... replicate?"

Mira held his gaze, carefully controlling her expression. "Replication would be difficult. Genetic markers like this are complex, and isolating them requires precision. But it's not impossible."

Lawson's smile was cold, calculated. "Good. Very good. Keep me updated on your progress, Dr. Kline. And remember—time is of the essence."

With that, he turned and left, leaving Mira alone with a sense of dread that settled heavily in her chest. She knew that Lawson's interest wasn't in a cure for the masses. He was interested in a way to control who received immunity—and, by extension, who survived.

She returned to her work with a renewed determination, her mind racing with the implications of her discovery. She would continue her research, but she would do so with caution.

There was too much at stake to allow her findings to be twisted into something monstrous.

The days that followed were a blur of experiments and late-night analysis sessions, as Mira and Jamie delved deeper into the genetic marker. Every discovery brought them closer to a viable immunity serum, but also closer to a truth Mira wished she could ignore. This marker—this tiny piece of genetic code—held the power to rewrite the future of humanity.

Finally, after days of tireless work, they synthesized the first test serum. Mira held the vial in her hands, its contents glowing faintly in the sterile light of the lab. It was a strange, beautiful thing, a beacon of hope and fear intertwined.

She looked at Jamie, who was watching her with a mixture of excitement and apprehension. "This is it," she said, her voice barely above a whisper. "The first step."

Jamie nodded, his eyes fixed on the vial. "But we need to be sure. If we're wrong..."

Mira took a deep breath, nodding. They couldn't afford any mistakes. This serum was more than a medical breakthrough—it was a choice, a decision about who would live and who would die. The weight of that responsibility bore down on her as she prepared to administer the first trial.

They selected a test subject from the immune group, a volunteer who had been closely monitored and was in stable condition. Mira carefully injected the serum, her hands steady but her heart pounding. As they watched, the subject's vitals remained steady, showing no signs of adverse reaction. After a tense half-hour, they observed a slight increase in immune response—a promising sign.

"It's working," Jamie said, his voice filled with quiet awe.

But Mira couldn't shake the unease that lingered in her mind. They had taken the first step, but the road ahead was fraught with peril. The serum was untested, and the consequences of its use—both intended and unintended—could be catastrophic.

As the days wore on, the initial success of the serum spurred them forward. They began expanding the trials, testing different dosages, refining the formula with each iteration. Word of their progress spread, and soon they found themselves under constant scrutiny, with military personnel and government officials monitoring their every move.

Mira knew that her research had become a weapon in its own right, a bargaining chip in the struggle for control over the virus. She felt trapped, caught between her duty as a scientist and her fear of what her discoveries would unleash.

One evening, as she reviewed the latest test results, Jamie approached her, his expression troubled.

"Mira," he said quietly, "we need to talk."

She looked up, sensing the urgency in his voice. "What is it?"

Jamie glanced around, as if afraid they were being watched. "I've been reviewing the data, looking at the potential applications of the serum. And... there's something you need to know."

He handed her a file, and Mira's heart sank as she scanned its contents. The data showed a secondary effect of the serum, one they hadn't anticipated. In certain individuals, the serum triggered an aggressive immune response that went beyond neutralizing the virus—it began attacking healthy cells, as if the immune system had been weaponized against the body itself.

"This... this could be deadly," Mira whispered, horror filling her voice. "We're talking about a serum that could turn people's own bodies against them."

Jamie nodded grimly. "And in the hands of someone like Lawson..."

Mira felt a wave of nausea wash over her. If Lawson and his associates knew about this effect, they would see it as an asset, not a flaw. They would have a serum that could both protect and destroy, a tool for selective survival on a genetic level.

She met Jamie's gaze, her voice shaking. "We can't let this happen. We can't let them use this serum as a weapon."

Jamie's face was set with determination. "Then we need to act. We need to find a way to disable the secondary effect, to make the serum safe for everyone."

They spent the next several nights working in secret, modifying the formula, hiding their progress from the watchful eyes of the military and government officials. Mira knew that if they were caught, the consequences would be severe, but she couldn't let fear deter her. She was fighting for more than just a cure—she was fighting for the right to protect life, to prevent her work from being perverted into a tool of destruction.

Finally, after days of painstaking adjustments, they created a new version of the serum, one that bypassed the deadly secondary effect. They tested it on themselves first, knowing that any adverse reaction would mean the end of their efforts. But to their relief, the serum was stable, showing no signs of the previous complications.

With a sense of triumph tempered by caution, Mira prepared to distribute the modified serum to the immune population, knowing that they were taking a step toward a world where immunity was not a weapon but a shared shield.

But as she stood in the lab, holding the vial that represented months of sacrifice and struggle, she knew their battle was far from over. The serum was safe—for now. But she had seen too much to believe that their fight was won. There would always be those who sought control, those who saw humanity as a genetic goldmine to be exploited.

As she injected the first volunteer with the modified serum, Mira whispered a silent promise: that she would protect her discovery, guard it from those who would misuse it, and ensure that her work remained a legacy of hope rather than a weapon of fear.

In that moment, as the volunteer's vitals remained stable and the serum took effect, Mira allowed herself a rare glimmer of optimism. They had created something powerful, something that could save lives. And as long as she drew breath, she would ensure that it stayed in the right hands.

Chapter 8: Moral Boundaries

Dr. Mira Kline sat in the sterile glow of the laboratory, staring at a vial of the serum she had spent months developing, her fingers grazing the glass as if it held answers to questions she hadn't dared to ask. The room was silent, the hum of equipment a distant murmur in the background, but inside her mind was a storm of voices, each one pulling her in a different direction. This serum—this cure—was the culmination of her life's work. It had the potential to save countless lives, to halt a pandemic that had torn through communities and countries alike. But now, in the stillness of her lab, she couldn't shake the feeling that the true battle was only beginning.

Two days ago, Mira had been summoned to a meeting with Colonel Isaac Lawson and several government officials, each one a suit-clad silhouette with eyes that revealed little but calculated purpose. The message was simple yet horrifying: they wanted her to tailor the serum for "selective immunity"—an immunity that could be administered to specific populations based on government discretion.

"It's for national security, Dr. Kline," Lawson had said, his voice smooth and unyielding. "We need to protect key personnel, essential leaders, individuals whose survival is critical to maintaining order. The pathogen has already destabilized too much. We can't afford further breakdown."

The officials had echoed his sentiment, nodding in agreement, their eyes focused on her with a mix of respect and expectation. They didn't see her as a person, she realized in that moment. She was a tool, a means to an end, a scientist who held the key to their survival strategy.

Mira had listened in stunned silence, her mind reeling as she struggled to comprehend what they were asking. It wasn't enough to stop the virus. They wanted to decide who lived and who died, to wield her serum as a weapon of control. Her discovery, her labor of love and sacrifice, was being twisted into something monstrous.

Now, sitting alone in her lab, Mira replayed the meeting in her mind, the words echoing like a taunt. *Selective immunity.* The phrase was a clinical veneer over a chilling reality: they wanted to create a future in which survival wasn't a right but a privilege, granted only to those deemed worthy by those in power. She couldn't stop thinking about the implications, the potential abuses, the lives that would be cut short simply because they hadn't made it onto the government's list.

As a scientist, Mira had always believed that knowledge was meant to serve humanity, to uplift and empower. But here, faced with the government's demands, she felt the weight of a decision she had never imagined she'd have to make. She had the power to say no, to refuse to comply, but the serum was her creation, and if she didn't control it, someone else would. She knew the government well enough to understand that they wouldn't hesitate to strip her of her work if she became an obstacle.

The door to her lab opened, breaking the silence. Jamie, her assistant and closest confidant, walked in, carrying a stack of files. He looked up, his face softening when he saw her expression.

"Mira, you okay?" he asked, setting the files down. "You look... troubled."

She hesitated, wondering how much she could share, how much Jamie could handle. But as she looked at him, she realized she didn't want to carry this alone.

"They want selective immunity, Jamie," she said quietly, her voice tinged with bitterness. "They want to choose who gets the serum, who gets to live."

Jamie's eyes widened, his face paling. "Wait—are you serious? Selective immunity? They can't be serious. That's... that's insane."

Mira nodded, her hands clenching into fists. "They're very serious. And they're willing to do whatever it takes to make it happen. They want me to create a version of the serum that can be tailored to specific genetic markers. They think that way they can control its distribution, ensure it only benefits those they deem 'essential.'"

Jamie shook his head, his voice filled with disbelief. "That goes against everything we've worked for, everything you stand for. This serum was supposed to be a cure, a solution for everyone. Not a tool for... for discrimination."

"I know," Mira replied, her voice strained. "But if I refuse, they'll just take my research, twist it to their will. They'll make sure it's done, with or without me. And if that happens, I lose any control over what they do with it."

Jamie fell silent, the weight of her words settling over him. Mira could see the conflict in his eyes, the same conflict raging within her. They were scientists, dedicated to knowledge, to healing, to making the world better. But now, they were being asked to cross a line, to sacrifice their principles for a cause they couldn't believe in.

"What are you going to do?" Jamie asked softly, his voice barely above a whisper.

Mira looked down at the vial in her hands, feeling its weight as if it were a stone tied to her conscience. She didn't have an answer, not yet. All she knew was that this decision would change everything—not just for her, but for the world.

"I don't know, Jamie," she replied, her voice hollow. "But I have to find a way to make this right."

Over the following days, Mira's life became a battleground of conflicting loyalties, a constant push and pull between her duty to humanity and the relentless pressure from the government. She found herself scrutinizing her work with a new perspective, trying to imagine how it could be twisted, how her serum could be weaponized. She examined every variable, every detail, searching for a way to protect her discovery from exploitation. But the more she studied it, the more she realized just how easily it could be manipulated.

The worst part, she discovered, was the knowledge that she was capable of doing what they asked. She had the skill, the expertise, the understanding to create a serum tailored to genetic markers, a serum that could be restricted to certain populations, withheld from others. It would be simple, elegant, a triumph of genetic engineering. And it would be an atrocity.

The thought haunted her, filling her with a sense of dread that grew with each passing day. She knew that the government was watching her closely, monitoring her progress, waiting for her to deliver what they wanted. She could feel their gaze like a shadow over her shoulder, a constant reminder that her work was no longer her own.

One evening, as she sat in her lab, exhausted and worn, Mira found herself questioning everything she had believed in. Was this the price of progress? The cost of discovery? Was it possible to create something pure, something good, without it being corrupted, twisted into a weapon?

She thought of her mentors, the scientists she had admired, the teachers who had inspired her to pursue this path. They had taught her to seek knowledge, to push the boundaries of science, to strive for a better world. But they had never warned her about this—about the moral quagmire, the ethical dilemmas, the dark side of innovation. They had never told her that one day she might be forced to choose between her ideals and her survival.

Mira's thoughts were interrupted by the sound of footsteps approaching her lab. She looked up, expecting to see Jamie, but instead found herself face to face with Colonel Lawson. He stood in the doorway, his expression unreadable, his eyes cold and calculating.

"Dr. Kline," he said, his tone deceptively polite. "I trust you've made progress on our request?"

Mira forced herself to remain calm, to keep her emotions in check. "I've been working on it," she replied, choosing her words carefully. "But it's a complex process. Creating selective immunity isn't as simple as flipping a switch. It requires a deep understanding of genetic markers, a level of precision that takes time."

Lawson nodded, though his patience seemed thin. "I understand that. But I must remind you, time is not a luxury we have. The country is in chaos, the world is on the brink. We need results, Dr. Kline. The longer this goes on, the more lives we lose."

Mira met his gaze, feeling a surge of anger rise within her. "Lives are already being lost, Colonel. People are dying because of this virus. And the solution isn't to play god with who gets to live and who doesn't. This serum was meant to save lives, not to serve as a tool for discrimination."

Lawson's eyes narrowed, a flicker of frustration crossing his face. "With all due respect, Dr. Kline, you're not seeing the bigger picture. This isn't about discrimination. It's about survival. We need a stable society, we need leadership, we need people who can hold the world together. This virus has already done enough damage. Our job is to preserve what's left."

"By choosing who deserves to be saved?" Mira shot back, unable to contain her anger. "By deciding that some lives are more valuable than others? That's not preservation, Colonel. That's a perversion of everything we stand for."

Lawson's expression hardened, his tone growing colder. "You're a scientist, Dr. Kline. Your job is to find solutions, not to moralize. We need you to stay focused on the task at hand. If you're unable to do that, we'll find someone who can."

The threat hung in the air, a stark reminder of the precarious position she was in. Mira clenched her fists, feeling a surge of helplessness. She wanted to fight back, to stand up to him, but she knew that defiance would only make things worse. They held all the power, all the control. She was just a scientist, a pawn in their game.

But as Lawson turned to leave, an idea began to form in Mira's mind, a glimmer of hope amidst the darkness. If they wanted her to create selective immunity, she would give them what they wanted. But she would do it on her terms.

Over the next few days, Mira worked tirelessly, crafting a plan that would allow her to fulfill the government's demands while still protecting the integrity of her work. She began developing a version of the serum that appeared to be selective, one that seemed tailored to certain genetic markers, but in reality, it was a decoy, a false trail that would buy her time.

In secret, she continued refining the original serum, working to make it accessible to all, to ensure that it couldn't be manipulated or restricted. She knew it was a risk, that if she were caught, the consequences would be dire. But she couldn't allow her work to become a tool of oppression, a means of dividing humanity.

One evening, as she was finalizing the decoy serum, Jamie approached her, his face filled with worry. "Are you sure about this, Mira? If they find out..."

"They won't," Mira replied, her voice steady. "They're looking for a way to control, not a cure. This decoy will keep them busy, make them think they're getting what they want. And in the meantime, we'll keep working on the real serum."

Jamie nodded, though the fear in his eyes remained. "You're risking everything."

"I know," Mira said quietly. "But it's a risk worth taking. If this serum falls into the wrong hands, if it's used to divide instead of heal... I won't let that happen."

Together, they continued their work, creating the decoy serum while refining the true formula. Mira knew that the path she had chosen was fraught with danger, that each day brought new risks. But she couldn't allow fear to dictate her actions. She had to believe that there was still a chance to make a difference, to ensure that her discovery served as a beacon of hope rather than a weapon of control.

As the days passed, Mira found herself growing more resolute, more determined. She had crossed a boundary, a line she had never thought she would cross, but she did so with a clear conscience. This was her stand, her fight, her legacy.

One morning, as she stood in the lab, staring at the vials of serum lined up before her, she felt a sense of peace. She had chosen her path, one defined not by fear or compromise, but by the principles she held dear.

And no matter what happened next, she knew she had done the right thing.

Chapter 9: Patient Consent

Dr. Mira Kline watched the group of immune survivors seated across from her in the clinical observation room, each person a testament to resilience and, perhaps more than they realized, to scientific discovery. They sat in a semicircle, some slouched in chairs, others looking warily around, expressions a mix of curiosity, wariness, and distrust. Mira couldn't blame them; they had been through a hellish journey—narrowly escaping the pathogen's grip only to find themselves subjected to endless tests and evaluations under a veil of secrecy. And now, Mira was beginning to wonder if the price of survival had grown too high for them, their autonomy eroded in pursuit of science.

The man to her left, Peter Nolan, was a firefighter who had watched his family fall one by one to the pathogen, leaving him the only survivor in his household. Beside him sat Carla Ruiz, a young mother who had contracted the virus while caring for her sick child; she too had miraculously survived, though her daughter had not. The others were similar stories—individuals who had been through unimaginable pain, yet found themselves here, in the hands of government scientists and military personnel, uncertain of what lay ahead.

As Mira looked at each of them, her thoughts drifted to her work, to the studies and genetic analyses she had undertaken. The discoveries were groundbreaking, with genetic markers isolated, sequences mapped, and immunity pathways identified. It was the kind of progress she had dreamed of making, the kind of science that could change the world. But beneath that scientific triumph lay a growing unease. These people weren't just data points or genetic specimens—they were human beings with stories, families, and dreams. And somewhere along the line, Mira feared she had started seeing them more as carriers of a genetic mystery than as people.

Clearing her throat, Mira stepped forward. "Thank you all for coming today," she began, her voice steady though her mind was racing. "I know you've been through a lot, and I want to acknowledge the strength each of you has shown. We're here today to go over the next steps in our research, and I want to make sure you understand everything that's happening. If you have any questions, please don't hesitate to ask."

Her words hung in the air, met with a few murmurs and nods. The tension in the room was palpable, a silent reminder of the mistrust that had begun to seep into every interaction. Mira knew that some of them resented the endless testing, the blood draws, the invasive procedures. She knew that every time she requested another sample or a scan, she was asking them to trust her, even though they were confined here under orders, with no real option to refuse.

Peter Nolan shifted uncomfortably in his chair. "Dr. Kline, when you say 'next steps,' what does that mean? Are you planning to do more tests? Because honestly, I don't think I can handle another round of blood draws."

Mira paused, taking in his words. "Yes, there will be more tests. But I'm hoping to keep them as non-invasive as possible. The purpose of these tests is to understand the genetic markers that made you immune to the pathogen. This knowledge could help us develop a cure or a vaccine."

Carla spoke up, her voice wavering. "And how much longer are we going to be here? It feels like we're prisoners. I have a life out there, Dr. Kline. I have family. I can't stay here forever."

Mira's heart twisted at her words. She knew Carla wasn't alone in feeling trapped, and she herself had questioned, time and again, whether they had crossed a line by holding these survivors. But every time she raised the issue with the officials, they insisted it was for the greater good, for "national security," as they liked to put it.

"I understand your concerns," Mira said, choosing her words carefully. "And I want to assure you that we're doing everything we can to speed up this process. But developing a cure takes time, and until we have a solution, I can't in good conscience release you all. If the virus mutates or resurfaces, you're among the few who can resist it. You're... essential to humanity's survival."

Peter's jaw tightened, his eyes narrowing. "That's what you keep saying, Dr. Kline. But it doesn't feel like survival when we're stuck in here like lab rats."

Mira felt her defenses waver. They had every right to feel this way. She had never intended for her work to infringe upon the lives of others, but the reality was far messier than she had ever anticipated. She had walked into this project with a sense of duty and purpose, only to find herself entangled in a web of ethical dilemmas that challenged everything she stood for.

She took a deep breath, steeling herself. "I want to make something clear. You are not prisoners. You are free to leave at any time, but I would strongly advise against it. There are risks, both to you and to others. If you were to carry the virus, or if we lose track of this immunity, it could lead to another outbreak. My goal isn't to keep you here against your will. I'm here to help you, to find a solution that will allow you to return to your lives safely."

The room fell silent, the survivors exchanging uneasy glances. Mira could see the mistrust lingering in their eyes, a doubt she knew wouldn't easily be dispelled. They were survivors, yes, but they had become something else in this place—subjects, specimens, pieces of a puzzle they hadn't chosen to be part of.

As the meeting ended, Mira lingered, watching as the survivors filed out of the room, their faces etched with weariness and resignation. She couldn't shake the feeling that she had failed them, that she was complicit in stripping them of their autonomy. They had survived a pandemic only to find themselves ensnared in a system that saw them as assets rather than individuals.

Later that evening, Mira sat alone in her office, staring at the data on her computer. Each genetic sequence, each marker she had identified, was a testament to their resilience, to the mysterious force that had protected them from the virus. But as she scrolled through the data, she felt a growing sense of discomfort. This information was powerful—too powerful—and in the wrong hands, it could be used to exploit these survivors in ways that made her stomach turn.

Just as she was about to shut down her computer, her assistant, Jamie, appeared at the door, looking uncharacteristically somber.

"Got a minute?" he asked, stepping into the room without waiting for an answer. Mira gestured for him to sit, sensing that he had something important on his mind.

Jamie cleared his throat, glancing around as if to make sure they were alone. "I've been reviewing the latest reports, and I... I came across something troubling."

Mira frowned, her pulse quickening. "What do you mean?"

Jamie handed her a file, his expression grim. "The government has been collecting additional data on the immune survivors. I didn't notice it at first, but they've been analyzing more than just their immunity. They're tracking behavioral patterns, psychological responses... it's as if they're looking for ways to predict compliance."

Mira felt a chill crawl up her spine as she flipped through the file, her eyes scanning the data Jamie had highlighted. The reports detailed behavioral analyses, noting which survivors were more "cooperative" and which ones exhibited "resistance." There were notes on Peter Nolan, labeling him as "hostile" and "potentially noncompliant," along with recommendations for increased monitoring.

"This is... disturbing," she whispered, her hands shaking slightly. "They're not just studying immunity. They're studying control."

Jamie nodded, his face pale. "I don't know how far it goes, but I'm worried, Mira. These people—they're not just immune survivors to the government. They're assets, resources to be managed. And if they don't comply... well, who knows what they'll do?"

Mira felt a surge of anger rise within her, a fury that burned away the doubt and fear that had been gnawing at her. She had dedicated her life to science, to the pursuit of knowledge, but she had never signed up for this. She hadn't sacrificed everything only to become part of a system that stripped people of their humanity.

"We can't let this happen," she said, her voice shaking. "These people—Carla, Peter, all of them—they deserve better than this. They deserve to be treated as human beings, not as assets."

Jamie hesitated, his eyes dark with worry. "Mira... if we go against the government, if we push back, there's no telling what they'll do. They won't just let us walk away."

Mira met his gaze, a fierce determination settling over her. "I know. But I can't stay silent. I can't sit by and watch as they turn these people into tools, as they strip them of their autonomy, their consent. If I do that, I'm no better than the pathogen we're fighting."

Together, they began devising a plan, a way to ensure that the survivors retained control over their own bodies, their own genetic data. It was risky, and Mira knew that if they were caught, the consequences would be severe. But she also knew that this was a fight worth taking.

Over the following days, Mira and Jamie worked in secret, encrypting the data, creating protocols that would give the survivors more control over their own information. They established a system for informed consent, ensuring that every test, every sample, was fully transparent and voluntary. And they made sure that each survivor had the option to refuse, to walk away without fear of reprisal.

One evening, as she was finishing up her work, Mira felt a sense of relief wash over her. For the first time in weeks, she felt like she was doing something right, something that honored the survivors' humanity rather than exploiting it.

But as she sat back, a sudden realization struck her—a chilling thought that made her heart race. The government wouldn't be satisfied with these new protocols. They would see her actions as defiance, as a threat to their control. And when they found out, they would come for her, for Jamie, and for anyone who dared to stand in their way.

She glanced at Jamie, who was typing furiously at his computer, his face set with determination. They had crossed a line, a line she knew they could never uncross. But she also knew that she couldn't stop now. The survivors deserved their autonomy, their right to control their own destinies. And Mira would do everything in her power to ensure that right was protected.

As she watched the survivors enter the lab the next day, each one looking at her with a newfound trust, Mira felt a sense of purpose she hadn't felt in a long time. She had chosen her path, one defined not by fear or compliance, but by a fierce commitment to justice.

But she also knew that the battle was far from over. The government would push back, they would try to reclaim control, to strip the survivors of the rights Mira had fought to protect. And when that day came, Mira would be ready.

In that moment, as she met Peter's gaze, she felt a sense of peace, a certainty that she had made the right choice. She had chosen to stand by the survivors, to honor their humanity, their resilience, and their right to control their own lives.

No matter what the government did, no matter how hard they fought to silence her, Mira knew that she would never stop fighting. She would protect these people, not as subjects, not as data, but as human beings.

And in doing so, she had found her purpose.

Chapter 10: The Cost of Knowledge

Dr. Mira Kline sat alone in her office, her fingers hovering over the keyboard as she stared at the sequence on the screen in front of her. The genetic data glowed faintly, a testament to months of tireless research, each segment representing a part of the immunity code she had been piecing together. She had unraveled much in her time working with the immune survivors, but this—this was something else. This discovery was the key to everything, the final piece in the puzzle of the pathogen, a blueprint that could save humanity from the brink of extinction. But as she stared at the data, a sense of dread coiled in her stomach, growing more intense with each passing second.

For all its promise, this knowledge was tainted. It was powerful, yes, but it was dangerous—more dangerous than she had ever anticipated. She had been so focused on unlocking the genetic mystery of immunity, on understanding what made certain people resistant to the virus, that she hadn't fully considered the implications. Now, standing at the precipice of discovery, she could see the costs as clearly as if they were written across her screen.

Her findings revealed more than immunity; they exposed a weakness within the human genome, a hidden vulnerability that the pathogen had exploited to spread so efficiently. The virus wasn't just a random mutation—it was a calculated, precision-engineered weapon, designed to latch onto this genetic Achilles' heel. And now, Mira had the means not only to halt it but also to manipulate it. If harnessed correctly, her research could allow her to reverse the effects of the virus, to make the immune protective traits accessible to everyone. But in the wrong hands, it could become a weapon of unfathomable power—a tool for selective survival, one that could decide the fate of millions based on genetic desirability.

Mira felt a shiver run down her spine as she considered the implications. The government had already pressured her to work on selective immunity, pushing for ways to control who received protection. If they knew about this breakthrough, they would see it as the ultimate advantage, a way to shape society according to their own designs. The thought made her stomach churn. She had not dedicated her life to science to see her work twisted into a weapon of control.

Lost in thought, she didn't hear Jamie enter the room. When he spoke, she jumped, startled out of her reverie.

"Long day, huh?" he asked, leaning against the doorframe, his face etched with concern. "I saw the lights on and figured you'd still be here."

Mira forced a smile, though it didn't reach her eyes. "Yeah, you could say that. I've... I've made some progress."

Jamie raised an eyebrow, sensing the hesitation in her voice. "Good progress or bad?"

She gestured to the screen, indicating the genetic sequence she had been analyzing. "Both. It's groundbreaking, Jamie. I've found a way to replicate the immune response. In theory, we could synthesize a treatment that would grant immunity to anyone."

Jamie's face lit up with excitement. "Mira, that's... that's incredible! Do you realize what this means? We could end this pandemic. You could be the one to save millions of lives."

But Mira shook her head, her expression grave. "It's not that simple. The implications are... staggering. This isn't just a cure, Jamie. It's a map, a guide to manipulating the very core of the human genome. With this knowledge, someone could do more than just cure the virus—they could reshape humanity."

The weight of her words hung in the air, and Jamie's smile faded, replaced by a look of unease. "You're saying it could be used as a weapon."

"Yes," Mira replied, her voice barely a whisper. "In the wrong hands, this discovery could be catastrophic. I didn't see it before—I was too focused on finding a cure, on understanding immunity. But now... I realize that this knowledge is more dangerous than the pathogen itself."

Jamie took a step back, processing her words. "So what do we do? Do we bury it? Pretend it doesn't exist?"

Mira shook her head, the conflict evident in her eyes. "I don't know. I can't just ignore it, Jamie. This is the culmination of everything I've worked for. But if I reveal it, there's no going back. The knowledge will be out there, and I won't be able to control how it's used."

They sat in silence for a moment, each lost in their thoughts. Mira felt the weight of her decision pressing down on her, suffocating her with its enormity. She had always believed that knowledge was a force for good, that science could be a tool for healing and progress. But now, she was forced to confront the darker side of discovery, the unintended consequences that came with pushing the boundaries of understanding.

After a long pause, Jamie spoke, his voice soft but resolute. "Mira, I know you. You've always been driven by the desire to help people, to make a difference. If anyone can find a way to use this knowledge responsibly, it's you."

Mira looked at him, a flicker of hope stirring in her chest. "Maybe. But even if I have the best intentions, there are people who would do anything to control this research, who would use it to further their own agendas. And I don't know if I can protect it from them."

Jamie hesitated, then placed a hand on her shoulder. "You don't have to do this alone. We'll figure it out together. Whatever it takes."

Mira felt a surge of gratitude, a warmth that eased the weight on her shoulders, if only for a moment. She knew the road ahead would be fraught with challenges, that she was walking a tightrope between discovery and destruction. But she also knew that she couldn't turn back. This knowledge, for better or worse, was hers to bear, and she would have to find a way to use it wisely.

Over the next few days, Mira immersed herself in her work, searching for a way to safeguard her discovery, to create a treatment that couldn't be weaponized or controlled. She experimented with different sequences, tested various delivery methods, hoping to find a solution that would grant immunity without opening the door to abuse. But each attempt brought new complications, new ethical dilemmas that forced her to question the very foundations of her research.

One afternoon, as she was deep in thought, Colonel Lawson entered the lab, his expression stern. Mira felt her heart skip a beat, a wave of anxiety washing over her. She had been avoiding him since her breakthrough, fearing that he might sense the change in her demeanor, that he might suspect she was withholding something.

"Dr. Kline," Lawson began, his tone clipped. "I've been reviewing your latest reports, and I noticed that progress has slowed. Is there a problem?"

Mira forced herself to remain calm, to hide the turmoil that simmered beneath the surface. "No, Colonel. The research is proceeding as expected. It's just... complex. There are a lot of variables to consider, and I want to make sure we get it right."

Lawson studied her, his gaze sharp. "I understand that, Dr. Kline. But we don't have the luxury of time. The pathogen is spreading faster than we anticipated, and we need a solution—now."

Mira felt a surge of anger at his words, at the relentless pressure he was placing on her. He didn't care about the ethical implications, about the dangers of her discovery. To him, this was a tool, a means to an end, and he would do whatever it took to see it realized.

"I'm doing everything I can, Colonel," she replied, her voice steady. "But science doesn't work on a timetable. If we rush this, we risk making mistakes, creating unintended consequences."

Lawson's eyes narrowed, a flicker of irritation crossing his face. "With all due respect, Dr. Kline, we don't have the luxury of worrying about 'unintended consequences.' The world is falling apart, and you're sitting on the solution. We need that cure, and we need it now. I suggest you expedite your efforts."

With that, he turned and left, leaving Mira alone, her hands clenched in frustration. She knew he was right, in a way. People were dying, and her research held the key to stopping the virus. But she couldn't shake the feeling that she was being backed into a corner, forced to make a decision that went against everything she believed in.

That night, Mira lay awake in her small quarters, her mind racing. She thought about her mentors, the scientists who had inspired her, who had taught her to respect the power of knowledge. They had always emphasized the importance of ethics, of responsibility, of considering the consequences of discovery. But none of them had prepared her for this—for the burden of knowledge, the weight of a discovery that held the potential to save humanity but at an immeasurable cost.

As she stared at the ceiling, Mira made a decision. She would move forward with her research, but she would do it on her own terms. She would find a way to protect her discovery, to ensure that it couldn't be twisted into something monstrous. And if that meant defying the government, risking her own safety, then so be it.

The next morning, Mira met with Jamie, outlining her plan. They would develop two versions of the serum: one that could be distributed widely, granting immunity without compromising genetic autonomy, and a second, decoy version that would satisfy the government's demands for control. It was a risky strategy, one that required precision and secrecy, but Mira was determined to see it through.

Over the following weeks, Mira and Jamie worked tirelessly, balancing their work with the constant scrutiny of Colonel Lawson and his team. They created layers of deception, encrypting data, hiding the true purpose of their research behind a facade of compliance. It was exhausting, nerve-wracking work, but it was the only way to ensure that their discovery remained in the right hands.

As the serum neared completion, Mira felt a sense of accomplishment tempered by a lingering unease. She had succeeded in creating a treatment that could save millions, a cure that would bring hope to a world on the brink of despair. But she knew that her fight was far from over. The knowledge she had uncovered, the secrets she had unlocked, would always be a target, a prize for those who sought power and control.

One evening, as Mira and Jamie reviewed the final data, a sense of quiet determination settled over her. She had chosen her path, one defined by responsibility and integrity, by a commitment to protect humanity rather than control it. And no matter what challenges lay ahead, she would remain steadfast in her mission.

As she looked at Jamie, she felt a sense of gratitude, a recognition of the sacrifices they had both made, the lines they had crossed in pursuit of a better future. They had walked a path fraught with danger, with moral ambiguity, but they had done so with the best of intentions, guided by a shared belief in the power of knowledge to heal rather than harm.

In that moment, Mira knew that she had found her purpose—not just as a scientist, but as a guardian of the truth, a protector of humanity's future. And as she prepared to take the final steps in her journey, she knew that the cost of knowledge was steep, but that it was a price worth paying.

Chapter 11: Power Brokers

Dr. Mira Kline stood by the window of her dimly lit lab, her gaze fixed on the skyline beyond the facility. The city, once a bustling metropolis, had transformed into a shadow of its former self, a hushed and uneasy landscape. Streets that had once teemed with people and life now lay silent and still, punctuated by the occasional sweep of searchlights from drones patrolling the perimeter. These were no longer days of innovation and discovery but of fear and exploitation, and Mira had come to realize that her discovery was at the heart of a new, darker era.

She had been haunted by the rumors trickling into the lab: whispers of negotiations, clandestine meetings, government pressures, and factions vying to control her work. She couldn't ignore the changes in Lawson's tone during his recent visits. He'd grown increasingly cold, his once-thin veneer of civility eroded by desperation, and his demands became more frequent, more urgent. The world outside, it seemed, was crumbling faster than she'd anticipated, and as immunity research became a strategic resource, power brokers from every corner of the globe had turned their gaze toward her lab.

Mira sighed, gripping the edge of her desk as she turned back to her screen. Her latest findings were sprawled across the monitor—a sea of complex genetic codes, carefully segmented and color-coded to show the differences between the immune and the susceptible. To her, it was a marvel of science, a discovery that could alter the fate of humanity, but to those outside, it was a ticket to control, a weapon, a currency with which to reshape the world.

The intercom on her desk crackled to life, and Jamie's voice broke through, tinged with urgency. "Dr. Kline, we have a situation. Colonel Lawson is here with... someone. I think you should come to the briefing room."

Her stomach tightened, a familiar dread settling over her. She'd heard rumors of this meeting—international delegations, private corporations, even biotech firms—each vying for exclusive access to her research. She'd done everything in her power to limit the dissemination of her findings, to protect the serum from becoming a weapon of greed, but it seemed the walls were closing in. Mira steeled herself, smoothing the lab coat over her shoulders as she headed toward the briefing room.

As she walked through the winding corridors, she couldn't shake the feeling that she was marching toward something irreversible, a point from which there would be no return. The doors to the briefing room opened with a quiet hiss, and Mira stepped inside, her gaze immediately drawn to the unfamiliar faces around the table. Lawson stood at the head, flanked by men and women in tailored suits, their expressions cold and calculating. Representatives from governments, private industries, defense contractors—all gathered here in the sterile confines of her lab, as if it were a stock exchange.

"Dr. Kline," Lawson greeted her, his voice carefully neutral. "Thank you for joining us. We have some new developments to discuss."

Mira nodded, her eyes scanning the room. She recognized a few faces from news reports—ambassadors, CEOs, high-ranking officials. There was something predatory in their gazes, as if they were already calculating the profits, the influence, the control they could wring from her work. She took a seat, folding her hands in front of her as she met Lawson's gaze.

"What's this about?" she asked, keeping her tone measured.

Lawson's mouth tightened into a semblance of a smile. "As you know, Dr. Kline, your research has attracted attention on a global scale. The immunity serum you've developed represents an unprecedented advancement in medical science, and naturally, there are parties interested in partnering with us to ensure its distribution."

Mira suppressed a scoff, her gaze hardening. "Distribution? Or control?"

One of the men, a sharp-eyed executive from a pharmaceutical giant, leaned forward, his fingers steepled beneath his chin. "Dr. Kline, let's be pragmatic. Your serum has the potential to change the course of human history. But it also poses challenges—production, distribution, logistical concerns. We have the resources, the networks, to make this a global success."

"A success," Mira repeated, her voice edged with disbelief. "Do you mean saving lives, or selling them immunity at a price?"

The executive's expression didn't waver, though Mira detected a flicker of annoyance. "We're here to offer assistance. The world is in chaos. People are desperate, and the right partnerships could ensure that this serum reaches those in need—while, of course, recouping some of the costs involved in such an enormous undertaking."

Mira felt the room grow colder as the man's words sank in. The immunity serum wasn't just a medical breakthrough to them—it was a commodity, a product with a price tag, a bargaining chip in a high-stakes game of power and profit. She glanced at Lawson, searching his face for any hint of remorse, but his expression was impassive, his loyalty to his superiors unwavering.

Another representative, a woman from a private defense contractor, spoke up, her voice smooth and confident. "Dr. Kline, we understand your concerns. But let's be clear—this serum could be used strategically, deployed in regions where stability is critical. Imagine the impact on the military, on government operatives, on those essential to maintaining order."

Mira clenched her fists beneath the table, fury boiling beneath her calm exterior. "You're talking about selective immunity. Choosing who gets to survive, who deserves protection. That's not science. That's... that's eugenics under another name."

The woman raised an eyebrow, her smile thin. "Call it what you like, Dr. Kline. But in times of crisis, hard choices must be made. The survival of civilization depends on stability, on protecting key assets. Your serum could be instrumental in ensuring that our society remains intact."

Mira felt as if the air had been sucked from the room. She had dedicated her life to understanding viruses, to harnessing the power of science for the greater good. And now, these people wanted to turn her work into a tool for division, a means to decide who was worthy of survival. She thought of the immune survivors she had worked with, people like Peter and Carla, who had endured unimaginable loss and suffering, only to find themselves pawns in a game they hadn't chosen to play.

Taking a steadying breath, Mira forced herself to remain calm. "The serum was developed to protect everyone, not just a select few. It's meant to be a shield, not a weapon."

Lawson's gaze sharpened, his voice cutting through the room. "Dr. Kline, the world isn't so simple. We're not in a position to hand out immunity like candy. Resources are limited. The infrastructure is collapsing. We have to prioritize, to make tough decisions."

Mira felt her anger flare, her voice rising. "This isn't about resources, Colonel. This is about control. You want to wield immunity as a bargaining chip, to trade lives for power. But people are dying, and you're turning this into a business deal."

The room fell silent, the tension palpable. Mira's heart pounded in her chest, but she held her ground, meeting each gaze with unwavering resolve. She had come too far, sacrificed too much, to see her work corrupted in this way. She knew that speaking out could cost her, that these people held more power than she could ever hope to counter. But she couldn't stay silent, couldn't let them twist her discovery into something monstrous.

One of the ambassadors, a man from a major world power, leaned forward, his voice calm but insistent. "Dr. Kline, let's not be idealistic. This isn't about exploitation. It's about survival. Humanity is at a tipping point. We're facing a crisis unlike anything we've ever seen, and your serum is the solution. But without cooperation, without structure, we're doomed to chaos."

Mira met his gaze, a steely determination settling over her. "If we start deciding who lives and who dies based on political alliances or profit margins, we've already lost our humanity. This serum should be accessible to all, without discrimination."

Lawson's expression hardened, his patience thinning. "And how do you propose we do that, Dr. Kline? How do you plan to distribute this serum to billions of people, to navigate the logistical nightmare of mass immunization without a framework in place?"

"We build a framework based on equity, on ethical distribution, not on profit or political gain," Mira shot back. "We partner with independent organizations, NGOs, public health agencies. We put people over politics."

The room erupted in murmurs, some of the representatives shaking their heads, others leaning in to confer with one another. Mira could see the resistance in their eyes, the unwillingness to relinquish their vision of a world controlled by selective immunity. To them, her words were naïve, a hindrance to their plans.

Lawson held up a hand, silencing the room. His gaze fixed on Mira, a chilling calm in his voice. "Dr. Kline, I respect your passion, but idealism won't save lives. This is the real world. And in the real world, hard decisions must be made. We're prepared to offer you resources, support, security—everything you need to make this serum a reality. But we need your cooperation."

Mira's jaw clenched, her resolve hardening. She had a choice to make, a decision that would define her legacy. She could yield to their demands, surrender her work to their control, and watch as her discovery became a tool for power and profit. Or she could fight, resist, protect her work from those who sought to corrupt it.

"I appreciate your offer, Colonel," she replied, her voice steady. "But I didn't come here to play politics. I came here to save lives. And if that means standing against all of you, then that's what I'll do."

Lawson's expression darkened, his tone laced with a warning. "Be careful, Dr. Kline. You're walking a dangerous path."

Mira held his gaze, refusing to back down. "I'd rather walk this path alone than betray the people this serum was meant to help."

The silence that followed was heavy, charged with tension. Mira could feel the weight of their stares, the unspoken threats lingering in the air. But she stood her ground, unyielding, a fierce determination blazing in her eyes.

As the meeting adjourned, the representatives filed out, each casting her a final, calculating glance. Lawson lingered, his gaze cold and unyielding.

"You're making a mistake, Dr. Kline," he said, his voice low. "You can't win this fight."

Mira met his gaze, her voice unwavering. "Maybe not. But I can't stand by and let you destroy everything I've worked for."

Lawson's jaw tightened, and without another word, he turned and left, leaving Mira alone in the empty room, the weight of her decision settling over her. She knew she had chosen a difficult path, one fraught with danger and uncertainty. But she also knew that she couldn't betray her principles, her commitment to humanity.

As she returned to her lab, Mira felt a newfound resolve, a fire ignited within her. She would protect her work, safeguard her discovery, even if it meant standing against the world. She had come too far, sacrificed too much, to let her discovery fall into the wrong hands.

In the quiet of the lab, surrounded by her research, Mira whispered a silent vow—a promise to protect the serum, to keep it from becoming a tool of exploitation, to ensure that her work served the people, not the powerful.

No matter the cost.

Chapter 12: The Underground Immunes

Dr. Mira Kline was hunched over her desk, lost in a labyrinth of data, when a quiet tap at her door broke her concentration. She looked up, surprised; she wasn't expecting anyone. It was past midnight, and by now, the lab was mostly empty. The few remaining staff who lingered this late were either military personnel or scientists under orders from Colonel Lawson. But Jamie was standing in the doorway, his face shrouded with an expression Mira had rarely seen on him—caution mixed with urgency.

"Jamie," she said, a note of concern creeping into her voice. "What's wrong?"

Jamie closed the door behind him, casting a quick glance around the room before he spoke. "Mira, I've found something. Something that changes everything." His voice was barely a whisper, yet it carried a weight that made Mira's heart skip a beat.

"What is it?" she asked, her curiosity piqued and her mind already racing with possibilities.

Jamie hesitated, his gaze intense. "I can't explain it here. We're not safe. There are too many ears in these walls."

Mira felt a surge of unease. Ever since her confrontation with Lawson and the foreign delegates, she had felt the invisible net of surveillance tighten around her. It wasn't unusual to catch a glimpse of security personnel stationed outside her lab or to notice that her digital logs and files seemed to be checked more frequently than usual. But Jamie's cryptic words took that paranoia to a new level.

"Let's go somewhere secure," she whispered, grabbing her coat and signaling for him to lead the way.

They navigated through the dimly lit hallways, moving quietly past the guard stations and checkpoints, until they reached a small storage room on the far side of the complex. Jamie slipped inside first, and once Mira joined him, he shut the door, flicking on the dim light. She noticed he was holding a small, pocket-sized device she hadn't seen him use before.

"A signal jammer," he explained, noticing her questioning look. "It'll block any nearby surveillance equipment. We should be safe here, at least for a few minutes."

He pulled a small tablet from his pocket, handing it to her. Mira's eyes widened as she scanned the screen, the images and text lighting up in the darkness. The file contained names, photographs, and reports from scattered locations—mostly cities on lockdown or regions the government considered to be pathogen hotspots. Each entry bore a brief description of an individual immune to the virus, along with a list of their known associates and suspected locations.

Mira looked up at Jamie, a mixture of disbelief and horror on her face. "Is this...?"

"An underground network of immunes," Jamie confirmed, his voice heavy. "They're avoiding detection, staying off the grid, resisting government capture. They know they're targets, and they're fighting back."

Mira's mind spun, struggling to process this revelation. She had long suspected that the immune survivors she'd studied were just a fraction of the total immune population, but she had assumed the others were either in hiding or unaccounted for in the chaos. The idea that they had organized, that they had banded together in defiance of the government, was both shocking and strangely inspiring.

"How did you find this?" she asked, her eyes scanning the file for familiar faces, though she hoped she wouldn't find any.

"I've been monitoring encrypted channels," Jamie replied, a flicker of pride in his voice. "There's a whole network—people communicating, sharing locations, warning each other about government raids. They've been keeping themselves hidden, moving between safe houses. And they're organized, Mira. They have contacts, resources... even a way of identifying other immunes without drawing attention."

Mira's pulse quickened. She was staring at the evidence of a grassroots resistance, a group of people who had defied the odds and refused to submit to the government's demands. They weren't just running—they were fighting back, reclaiming their autonomy, their freedom, and their right to live without becoming subjects in a lab.

"This is incredible," Mira whispered, her mind racing with possibilities. "These people—they're the key to understanding the true scope of immunity. If they've managed to stay hidden, that means they've been able to resist government capture, evade the testing, the surveillance..."

"And they're not just hiding," Jamie added, a note of admiration in his voice. "They're helping others, too. People in these files have been providing safe passage for immune refugees, moving them across state lines, sometimes even across borders. It's like they're creating a network of resistance. They're... they're building something no one else could."

Mira felt a rush of emotion—hope mixed with pride. The immunes she had studied had all been victims, people stripped of their freedom and treated like assets. But this network was something different, something alive. It represented the spirit of resistance, the refusal to be controlled, the fight for survival on their own terms.

But that hope was tempered by a harsh reality. "If the government finds out about this... if Lawson finds out..."

Jamie nodded, his face grave. "They'll come down on them with everything they've got. This kind of defiance won't go unnoticed. They'll see it as a threat, an affront to their control."

Mira bit her lip, weighing her options. She knew that exposing this network could jeopardize everything, could lead to widespread crackdowns and more aggressive tactics to capture and control the immune. But she also knew that these people represented a path forward, an opportunity to study immunity outside the constraints of government oversight. If she could connect with them, learn from them, maybe she could find a way to distribute the serum without it falling into the hands of those who sought to weaponize it.

"Jamie," she said, her voice resolute. "We need to make contact. We need to find a way to reach these people, to let them know that they're not alone."

Jamie's eyes widened. "You want to join them?"

"Not join," she replied, shaking her head. "But we need to understand them. They have something that we don't—freedom, independence. And if we can gain their trust, if they're willing to help us... this could be the key to distributing the serum without it becoming another weapon for the powerful."

Jamie hesitated, glancing down at the tablet. "It's a risky move, Mira. If Lawson finds out..."

"He won't find out," she said firmly. "We'll be careful. We'll use secure channels, keep our communications encrypted. But we can't sit back and do nothing. These people are the embodiment of what we've been fighting for—autonomy, freedom, the right to live without fear. They're the proof that immunity isn't just a genetic anomaly. It's a power, a strength that can be used for good."

Jamie nodded slowly, his eyes meeting hers. "Then let's do it. But we need to proceed with caution. I'll set up a secure line, one that Lawson and his team won't be able to trace. And... there's something else."

Mira raised an eyebrow, sensing his hesitation. "What is it?"

Jamie took a deep breath, his expression conflicted. "I think we need someone on the inside. Someone who can bridge the gap, who can earn their trust. If we send a message out of nowhere, they'll be suspicious. But if we have an envoy, someone who can vouch for us... it might make all the difference."

Mira considered his words, realizing the truth in them. The underground immunes had built a network of trust, forged through shared struggle and survival. If she wanted to reach them, she would need someone who could break through the walls of suspicion, someone who understood their plight.

"Who do you have in mind?" she asked, already suspecting the answer.

Jamie hesitated, then spoke the name that had been on her mind since the beginning. "Peter Nolan."

Mira felt a pang of sadness as she thought of Peter, the firefighter who had lost everything to the virus, a man whose strength and resilience had impressed her from the beginning. He had been one of the first immune survivors she had studied, and despite his resentment toward the government and its endless tests, he had always complied, never once asking for special treatment or complaining about the invasions of privacy.

"He's perfect," she said softly. "But he won't be easy to convince. He's already sacrificed so much."

Jamie nodded, his face somber. "I know. But if anyone can reach these people, it's him. He's been through it all—the losses, the fear, the testing. And he's trusted by the others. They look up to him. If we can convince him to go, to be our voice... he might be able to do what we can't."

Mira took a deep breath, steeling herself for the conversation ahead. She knew it wouldn't be easy, that asking Peter to leave the relative safety of the lab and infiltrate an underground network of immunes was a dangerous request.

But if there was a chance, even a small one, that he could bridge the gap, she had to try.

"Let's talk to him," she said, her voice filled with determination. "But we'll leave it up to him. I won't force him into this. He deserves the choice."

Jamie nodded, and together, they left the storage room, the weight of their plan settling over them. Mira knew that this was a turning point, a decision that would shape the future of her work, her legacy, and the lives of those she sought to protect. She had entered this journey with the hope of finding a cure, of saving lives. But now, she realized, she was fighting for something much deeper—a battle for autonomy, for freedom, for the right to live without being controlled.

As they approached Peter's quarters, Mira felt a surge of resolve, a fire ignited within her. She would do whatever it took to reach the underground immunes, to protect them, to stand with them in their fight for freedom.

And she knew, as she knocked on Peter's door, that there was no turning back.

Mira waited, her breath steady but her heart racing, as the seconds ticked by before Peter's door finally opened. He stood in the threshold, his eyes weary but alert, looking at her and Jamie with a hint of suspicion.

"Dr. Kline? Jamie? It's late. What's going on?" His voice was low, tinged with caution, but there was no hostility in his tone.

Mira offered him a reassuring smile, though she knew what she was about to ask of him might test his patience—and his trust. "Peter, we need to talk. It's important, and I'm afraid we can't wait until morning."

Peter studied her for a moment, then stepped aside, motioning for them to enter. Mira walked in, taking a seat in the modest, dimly lit room. Jamie followed, casting a quick glance at Peter, as if assessing his state of mind.

Once they were all settled, Mira took a deep breath and looked directly at Peter. "I want to share something with you. It's information we haven't been able to discuss openly because... well, there's a lot at stake."

Peter's gaze hardened slightly, and Mira could see a flicker of mistrust. "Sounds like more secrets. I thought we were past that, Dr. Kline."

Mira nodded, feeling the sting of his words but understanding their weight. "I understand, Peter. And you have every right to feel that way. But please, let me explain. We've discovered something—a network of immune individuals who are actively resisting the government's efforts to control them. They're staying off the radar, helping each other, building a community where they can live freely, outside of government reach."

Peter's eyes narrowed as he absorbed her words. "An underground network? And you're telling me this because...?"

Mira looked at Jamie, who gave her a slight nod. She took a steadying breath before continuing, aware that this next part could either gain Peter's cooperation or drive him further away.

"We want to reach them, Peter. We believe that connecting with this network could help us distribute the serum without it becoming another weapon for those in power. They represent hope—people who won't be controlled, who are finding ways to survive on their own terms. If we can connect with them, we could save lives without putting immunity in the hands of those who want to use it for control."

Peter was silent, his expression unreadable. He looked down, his fingers clenching slightly as he processed what she had said. When he finally spoke, his voice was measured, tinged with both anger and sadness.

"So, you're asking me to leave here, to go underground, and put my life on the line to meet these people? Do you understand what you're asking, Dr. Kline? I've already lost everything—my family, my home. And now you're asking me to risk what little I have left for a network of strangers?"

Mira's heart ached at his words, and she felt the weight of what she was asking him to do settle heavily on her shoulders. She knew she was asking him to make a tremendous sacrifice, one that few would be willing to consider. But she also knew that he was the only one who could do this—who could break through to these people and convince them to trust her and Jamie.

"Peter," she said softly, her voice filled with compassion, "I know what I'm asking of you is difficult, perhaps even unfair. But I believe in you. I believe that you can help us make a difference, that you can be the bridge between this lab and the people who need our help. And if there's any chance that we can protect the immune from being controlled, from being exploited... isn't that worth fighting for?"

Peter met her gaze, and she could see the struggle in his eyes. He was torn, wrestling with conflicting loyalties, his desire for freedom battling with his desire to make a difference. He had been through so much, and now she was asking him to take on yet another burden, to put himself in harm's way once more.

Finally, he spoke, his voice thick with emotion. "What makes you think they'll listen to me? What makes you think they'll even trust me?"

Mira looked at him earnestly. "Because you understand them, Peter. You've lived through what they're living through. You know what it feels like to be treated as an asset, to be stripped of your freedom. You can connect with them in a way that I never could. And I believe that if you speak from the heart, if you show them that we're not just another group trying to control them, they'll listen."

Peter sat back, his shoulders sagging as he mulled over her words. He glanced at Jamie, then back at Mira, searching their faces for any sign of deception, any hint that this might be another trap. But all he saw was sincerity, a genuine desire to protect those who had been cast aside by society, those who had fought to survive on their own terms.

After a long pause, he finally nodded, though his expression remained wary. "Fine. I'll go. But I'm doing this on my terms. No strings, no hidden agendas. If I get even the slightest hint that this is some kind of setup, I'm gone. And if I decide that these people aren't interested, that they don't want our help, I'm walking away."

Mira felt a surge of relief and gratitude, a weight lifting from her chest. "Thank you, Peter. I promise, we'll give you as much support as we can. You'll have secure channels to reach us, and we'll provide any resources you need."

Peter nodded, though his expression remained guarded. "Then let's get this over with."

The next few days were a whirlwind of preparation. Jamie worked tirelessly to create a secure communication line, one that wouldn't be traceable by Lawson or any of the government's surveillance networks. Mira gathered supplies for Peter, including medical kits, encrypted devices, and a portable jammer to block tracking signals. Every detail had to be perfect—any misstep, any oversight, could mean the difference between success and failure.

As they prepared, Mira found herself growing both hopeful and anxious. She knew that Peter was taking a tremendous risk, that he was stepping into uncharted territory with nothing but their trust to guide him. But she also knew that he was strong, resilient, and determined, and she believed that he could succeed where others might fail.

On the morning of his departure, Mira met Peter in a quiet corner of the lab, away from prying eyes. She handed him a small, unmarked satchel filled with supplies, her expression a mixture of concern and determination.

"Are you sure you're ready for this?" she asked, her voice soft.

Peter gave a faint smile, though there was no warmth in it. "As ready as I'll ever be. Besides, if this goes south, it's not like I have much to lose."

Mira's heart ached at his words, but she didn't press him. She knew that he was carrying a heavy burden, that he was stepping into a world filled with uncertainty and danger. All she could do was offer her support and hope that he would find a way to make contact with the underground immunes.

"Good luck, Peter," she said, her voice filled with sincerity. "And remember—you're not alone. We're here, every step of the way."

Peter nodded, his gaze steady. "I'll keep that in mind."

With one final glance, he turned and disappeared into the shadows, leaving Mira standing alone in the quiet of the lab. She watched him go, a mixture of pride and anxiety filling her heart. She had placed her trust in him, had sent him on a mission that could change the course of their fight for freedom. And now, all she could do was wait and hope that he would find a way to reach the underground, to bridge the gap between the lab and the world beyond.

Peter traveled for days, moving through abandoned cities, deserted highways, and back roads, following leads that Jamie had uncovered through encrypted channels. Each step brought him closer to his destination, but it also heightened his sense of vulnerability, the awareness that he was alone, far from the relative safety of the lab.

Finally, after what felt like an eternity of traveling, Peter found himself standing in front of an old, nondescript building on the outskirts of a ghost town. The address matched the one Jamie had given him—a supposed safe house for the underground immune network. Peter took a deep breath, steeling himself for what lay ahead, then pushed open the door and stepped inside.

The room was dimly lit, with only a few flickering candles casting shadows across the walls. A group of people sat huddled together, their faces wary as they looked up to see him. There was an air of tension in the room, a quiet, simmering fear that spoke of lives spent on the run, of a constant battle for survival.

One of the men stood, his expression hard as he sized up Peter. "Who are you?"

Peter met his gaze, his voice steady. "My name is Peter Nolan. I'm immune. I came here... because I heard you're helping people like me. People who don't want to be controlled."

A murmur rippled through the group, and the man's expression softened slightly, though he remained guarded. "How did you find us?"

Peter hesitated, choosing his words carefully. "I have contacts. People who want to help, who believe that the immunes deserve freedom, not control. They sent me here to find you, to see if there's a way we can work together."

The man studied him, his gaze sharp. "And why should we trust you? For all we know, you could be working for the government, sent here to betray us."

Peter took a step forward, his voice filled with quiet conviction. "I've lost everything to this virus. My family, my friends... all gone. I know what it's like to be hunted, to be treated like an asset instead of a human being. I came here because I believe in what you're doing. Because I want to be free, just like you."

The man watched him for a moment, his expression unreadable. Then, with a nod, he gestured for Peter to sit, the tension in the room easing slightly.

"Welcome to the underground," he said quietly. "But remember—trust is earned, not given. You'll have to prove yourself."

Peter nodded, understanding the unspoken challenge in the man's words. He knew that he was entering a world of secrecy and suspicion, a world where survival depended on trust forged through shared struggle. But he also knew that he had found his place, that he was among people who understood his pain, his anger, his desire for freedom.

As he sat among the immunes, listening to their stories, their plans, their hopes for a life free from control, he felt a surge of purpose. He had come here as a messenger, a bridge between worlds, but he realized that he had found something deeper—something worth fighting for, worth sacrificing for.

And he knew, as he looked into their determined faces, that he would do whatever it took to protect them.

Chapter 13: A Question of Loyalty

Dr. Mira Kline sat alone in her office, the glow from her computer screen casting shadows across her face. The weight of the past few weeks was beginning to show in her features—the deep lines of fatigue etched into her brow, the shadows under her eyes that seemed to grow darker with each passing day. She had been at the forefront of an extraordinary discovery, one that could change the course of history. But what she hadn't anticipated was the immense burden it would place on her conscience, the constant tug-of-war between duty, ethics, and an emerging loyalty she hadn't foreseen.

The knock at her door broke her out of her thoughts. She looked up to see Jamie, her steadfast assistant, standing in the doorway. His face was tight with concern, his eyes wary.

"Mira," he said, his voice barely above a whisper, "we need to talk."

Mira gestured for him to come in, feeling a surge of relief at the sight of a familiar face. Jamie was one of the few people she could still trust, a grounding presence in the chaotic world her lab had become. As he closed the door behind him and took a seat across from her, she could see the tension in his expression, the same inner conflict she'd been grappling with.

"They're pushing harder," Jamie began, his tone grave. "Lawson came by earlier. He wanted to know if we'd made any progress with the serum modifications."

Mira's stomach tightened. She knew what he was referring to—the "selective immunity" program Lawson had been pushing, a project that would allow the government to control who received the immunity serum and who didn't. It was a violation of everything she stood for, a blatant disregard for the ethical principles that guided her work. But Lawson's demands had become increasingly insistent, his threats veiled in polite suggestions and ultimatums that grew harder to ignore.

"I haven't given him any updates," Mira said, her voice low. "But I don't know how much longer I can keep stalling. They're watching me, Jamie. Every move I make, every file I access, it's all under surveillance. If I don't produce results soon, they'll start asking questions."

Jamie nodded, his expression grim. "I know. But there's something else." He paused, hesitating before continuing. "I heard rumors... about Peter."

Mira's heart skipped a beat. Since sending Peter into the underground network of immunes, she had been waiting anxiously for news, for some sign that he had managed to make contact. The thought that he might be in danger, that he might have been discovered by Lawson or the government's operatives, was a constant source of worry.

"What did you hear?" she asked, her voice barely above a whisper.

Jamie glanced around, as if making sure they were truly alone, before leaning in. "Apparently, Lawson got word of a resistance movement forming among the immunes. He thinks it's a direct threat to government stability, that they're plotting to disrupt the immunization program. He's ordered a crackdown on anyone suspected of harboring immunes outside of government control."

Mira's blood ran cold. She had known that sending Peter into the underground would be dangerous, that he was risking everything to make contact with the immunes who had managed to evade government capture. But she hadn't anticipated the lengths Lawson would go to silence any hint of dissent. This wasn't just a matter of security for him—it was a question of control, of ensuring that the government held all the power over who lived and who didn't.

"What does that mean for us?" Mira asked, her voice tight with fear.

Jamie hesitated, his gaze filled with sympathy. "It means that if they catch wind of what we're doing—if they find out we've been working with the underground—they'll shut us down. And they won't hesitate to go after you, Mira. You're too valuable to them. They'll force you to comply."

Mira felt a wave of nausea wash over her. She had known the risks, had understood that defying Lawson's orders would come at a price. But now, faced with the reality of what could happen, she found herself questioning the path she had chosen. Was she prepared to sacrifice everything—her career, her freedom, her life—for the sake of a principle? Could she really stand against the government, against the people who held her future in their hands?

And then there was Peter. She had sent him into the underground, trusting him to make contact with the immunes, to bridge the gap between the lab and the world outside. If he was caught, if Lawson discovered his involvement, he would bear the brunt of her decisions. The thought was almost unbearable, a weight pressing down on her chest with crushing force.

"I don't know what to do, Jamie," she admitted, her voice barely audible. "I feel like I'm being pulled in two directions. If I give in to Lawson, if I let him control the serum, I'm betraying everything I believe in. But if I keep resisting, if I keep working with the underground... I'm putting everyone at risk."

Jamie reached across the desk, his hand covering hers in a gesture of comfort. "You don't have to make this decision alone, Mira. Whatever you choose, I'll be with you. But I think you need to ask yourself—who are you really loyal to? The government? Your research? Or the people who depend on you?"

Mira felt a surge of emotion, a swell of gratitude for Jamie's support, even as her mind raced with the implications of his question. Who was she loyal to? She had always considered herself a scientist first, driven by a duty to pursue knowledge and improve the lives of others. But now, she was faced with a moral dilemma that went beyond the confines of the lab, a question that forced her to confront the very essence of her values.

As Jamie left, Mira sat alone in her office, the quiet of the lab pressing in around her. She thought about the people who had placed their trust in her—the immune survivors she had studied, the underground network fighting for their freedom, even Peter, who had risked his life to make contact with them. They were all counting on her to make the right choice, to use her knowledge for good rather than letting it become a tool of control.

But loyalty was a complicated thing, tangled in layers of responsibility, obligation, and trust. She had given years of her life to the government, had dedicated herself to the pursuit of science under its funding and protection. And now, she was standing at a crossroads, forced to choose between that loyalty and the people she had come to see as allies, as friends.

The days that followed were a blur of sleepless nights and agonizing decisions. Lawson's pressure continued to mount, his demands growing more insistent with each passing day. He wanted results, and he wanted them fast, and Mira could feel the noose tightening around her. She knew that her time was running out, that she would have to make a choice soon or risk losing control over her work entirely.

Finally, unable to bear the weight of her uncertainty any longer, Mira made a decision. She would go to the underground herself, would see firsthand what Peter had found, would speak with the immunes and try to understand their struggle. If she was going to risk everything, she needed to be certain, needed to see with her own eyes what was at stake.

Under the cover of darkness, Mira slipped out of the lab, her heart pounding as she made her way through the quiet streets. Jamie had given her the address of a safe house, a location where she could make contact with the underground without drawing attention. She moved quickly, her footsteps silent as she navigated the shadows, the weight of her decision pressing down on her with each step.

When she arrived at the safe house, a modest, nondescript building on the outskirts of the city, she was greeted by a young woman with piercing eyes and a guarded expression. The woman introduced herself as Lila, a member of the underground network, and led Mira inside, guiding her through a maze of dimly lit hallways until they reached a small, secure room at the back of the building.

Peter was waiting for her, his face etched with fatigue but his eyes alight with a determination she hadn't seen before. He stood as she entered, his expression unreadable as he took in the sight of her, a mixture of surprise and relief flashing across his face.

"Mira," he said, his voice rough with exhaustion. "I didn't expect to see you here."

Mira managed a faint smile, feeling a surge of gratitude for his presence. "I needed to see for myself, Peter. I needed to understand what we're fighting for."

Peter nodded, his expression softening. "Then you came to the right place."

He led her through the safe house, introducing her to the people who had become his allies, his family. They were a diverse group—men and women of all ages, each one marked by the experiences they had endured, each one carrying the scars of a life spent in hiding. They spoke of their struggles, their losses, their fears, but also of their hopes, their dreams of a world where they could live without being hunted, where they could raise their children without fear of government interference.

As Mira listened, she felt her heart break for them, felt the weight of their stories settle over her like a shroud. These were people who had done nothing wrong, who had simply survived, yet they had been cast out, treated as threats rather than as human beings. And now, they were fighting not only for their own freedom but for the freedom of others, for a chance to live on their own terms.

By the time she returned to the lab, Mira knew what she had to do. Her loyalty was no longer to the government, no longer to the institution that had funded her work and demanded her obedience. Her loyalty was to the people she had met, to the underground network that had welcomed her, to the immune survivors who had placed their trust in her.

The next morning, she met with Jamie, her voice steady as she outlined her plan. They would continue their work, but they would do so on their own terms, using the lab as a cover while secretly coordinating with the underground to distribute the serum. It was a risky, dangerous endeavor, one that could cost them everything if they were discovered. But Mira was resolute. She would not let her discovery be twisted into a tool of control, would not let it become a weapon in the hands of those who sought power over others.

As they worked, Mira felt a newfound sense of purpose, a clarity that had been missing for so long. She knew that the path she had chosen was fraught with danger, that the cost of her decision could be high. But she also knew that it was the right choice, that she was fighting not for herself but for a cause greater than any one person.

In the end, loyalty was not about obligation or duty. It was about trust, about standing by the people who had placed their faith in her, about using her knowledge to protect rather than control. And as she looked at Jamie, at the underground network she had come to see as her allies, Mira knew that she had finally found her true purpose, her true loyalty.

She would fight for them, for their freedom, for their right to live without fear. And no matter the cost, she would not let them down.

Chapter 14: The Cure Dilemma

Dr. Mira Kline's hands shook as she stared at the screen, the data on her monitor swimming before her eyes. It was a moment she had anticipated for years—a breakthrough so monumental it could alter the fate of humanity. But instead of elation, Mira felt an overwhelming sense of dread settle over her, a chill that seeped into her bones and made her question everything she thought she knew.

The lab was silent, save for the low hum of machinery, the sterile glow of fluorescent lights casting shadows across the walls. The air was thick with anticipation, the weight of the discovery pressing down on her shoulders like a heavy mantle. For months, Mira and her team had worked tirelessly, pushing the boundaries of science, chasing a cure that had always seemed just out of reach. And now, after countless hours of experimentation, sleepless nights, and ethical quandaries, they were closer than ever. The answer was within her grasp—a serum that could immunize the global population, a cure that would finally end the pathogen's devastating reign.

But it came with a cost.

The results were clear, irrefutable: to create a scalable cure, they would need a specific set of antibodies that only existed in the blood of certain immune individuals. These antibodies were unique, impossible to synthesize, the product of genetic anomalies that had somehow enabled a handful of people to resist the pathogen. Without these antibodies, the serum would be ineffective—a cure in theory but useless in practice.

Mira's mind raced, grappling with the implications of what she was seeing. She understood what this meant. The antibodies would need to be harvested, extracted from the immune survivors she had come to know and care for. And the process wasn't just a simple blood draw; it was invasive, grueling, a procedure that would leave those individuals vulnerable, weakened. For some, it could even be fatal.

The lab door creaked open, and Jamie stepped in, his face lined with exhaustion but lit with a faint glimmer of hope. He had been by her side since the beginning, a steadfast ally, his loyalty unwavering even as the challenges mounted. She looked up at him, her expression haunted, and he stopped, sensing the turmoil that swirled within her.

"Mira," he began cautiously, moving closer, "is everything okay? You said you found something."

Mira forced herself to nod, though her voice was strained. "Yes. We've found it, Jamie. The key to the cure. It's... it's in the immune individuals, in their antibodies. We were right all along. Their blood holds the answer."

Jamie's face lit up, and for a brief moment, Mira saw the spark of hope that had kept them going through the darkest times. "That's incredible, Mira! This could change everything. We could finally put an end to this nightmare."

But as he looked at her, his excitement faded, replaced by a look of concern. He could see the conflict in her eyes, the weight of a decision that went beyond science, beyond the bounds of reason and logic.

"What's wrong?" he asked, his voice soft, his eyes searching hers. "We've worked so hard for this. Why don't you seem... relieved?"

Mira took a deep breath, her hands clenching and unclenching as she tried to steady herself. "Because this cure isn't without consequences, Jamie. The antibodies we need... they can't be synthesized. They have to be taken directly from the immune individuals."

Jamie's face fell, the realization dawning on him as he processed her words. "You mean... we'd have to use them as donors?"

Mira nodded, her heart heavy. "Yes. And the procedure isn't safe. It would weaken them, potentially leave them vulnerable to the very pathogen they survived. Some might not make it through. We're talking about sacrificing a few to save the many."

The words hung in the air, a painful truth neither of them wanted to acknowledge. Mira felt the weight of it pressing down on her, suffocating her, a moral burden she hadn't anticipated. She had devoted her life to protecting others, to healing, to making the world a better place. But now, she was faced with a decision that went against everything she believed in, a choice that would force her to weigh the value of individual lives against the greater good.

"I can't do it, Jamie," she whispered, her voice choked with emotion. "I can't look these people in the eyes and tell them they have to sacrifice themselves. They've been through so much already—loss, pain, betrayal. How can I ask them to give up the one thing they have left?"

Jamie placed a hand on her shoulder, his expression somber. "I understand, Mira. But you know as well as I do that without those antibodies, the cure is useless. If we don't go through with this... more people will die. We're talking about millions, maybe even billions of lives."

Mira's gaze dropped to the floor, her mind racing as she tried to reconcile her sense of duty with her ethical convictions. She knew Jamie was right, that the stakes were unimaginably high. But the idea of sacrificing even a handful of immune individuals felt like a betrayal, a violation of the trust she had worked so hard to earn.

As she grappled with the decision, her thoughts drifted to the people she had come to know during her research—Peter, Carla, the underground network of immunes who had fought so hard to remain free. She thought of their stories, their resilience, the way they had defied the odds to survive. They were more than just test subjects; they were human beings, individuals who had faced unimaginable hardship and emerged stronger.

And now, she was being asked to put their lives on the line, to use them as instruments in the pursuit of a cure.

Mira turned to Jamie, her voice resolute. "We have to tell them the truth. We can't make this decision for them. They deserve to know what's at stake, to understand the risks, and to choose for themselves."

Jamie looked at her, his eyes filled with a mixture of admiration and apprehension. "You're right, Mira. They deserve to know. But are you prepared for what they might say?

If they refuse... we'll have no choice but to go back to square one."

Mira nodded, her jaw set. "I know. But I'd rather lose the chance at a cure than compromise my integrity. If we're going to do this, we're going to do it the right way. With honesty, with respect, with consent."

Later that afternoon, Mira called a meeting with the immune survivors who had volunteered for her research. They gathered in the observation room, a small group of individuals who had endured countless tests, procedures, and sacrifices in the hope that their immunity could lead to a breakthrough. Mira looked at each of them, her heart heavy as she prepared to deliver the news that would change everything.

Peter stood at the front of the group, his arms crossed, his expression wary but curious. Carla was beside him, her gaze fixed on Mira with a mixture of hope and apprehension. The others shifted uneasily, sensing the gravity of the moment, their eyes filled with questions they were too afraid to voice.

Mira took a deep breath, steeling herself. "Thank you all for coming. I know you've given so much already, and I want you to know how grateful I am for your willingness to help. We've made a breakthrough, a discovery that could lead to a cure. But there's something you need to know."

The room fell silent, the air thick with anticipation as they waited for her to continue. Mira's gaze swept over them, taking in their faces, the exhaustion and determination that marked each one.

"The cure we've developed requires a specific set of antibodies," she began, her voice steady but laced with sorrow. "Antibodies that only exist in the immune individuals.

Without them, the serum won't work. It's the final piece of the puzzle, the key to making this cure effective. But there's a cost."

She paused, her throat tight, and the weight of her words settled over them like a heavy fog.

"These antibodies can't be synthesized. They have to be taken directly from your blood. And the process... it's invasive. It would weaken you, make you vulnerable, potentially even expose you to the pathogen again. For some of you, it could be fatal."

A murmur rippled through the room, a mixture of shock and disbelief. Carla's face paled, her hand flying to her mouth as she processed the implications of what Mira was saying. Peter's jaw tightened, his gaze hardening as he realized the choice that lay before them.

Mira swallowed, her voice trembling as she continued. "I'm not asking you to make a decision right now. But I want you to understand the risks. This is a choice only you can make. I can't—and won't—force any of you to go through with this. You've been through enough already, and you deserve the right to decide for yourselves."

The silence that followed was deafening, each individual grappling with the weight of Mira's words. Some looked away, their expressions a mixture of fear and resignation, while others met her gaze, their eyes filled with a steely determination.

Peter was the first to speak, his voice rough but steady. "So, what you're saying is that we could be the cure, but we have to put ourselves on the line? We survived once, and now you're asking us to risk it all over again?"

Mira met his gaze, her heart aching at the pain in his voice. "Yes, Peter. That's exactly what I'm asking. And I know it's not fair. I wish there were another way, a way to create the cure without putting any of you at risk. But this is the reality we're facing."

Carla looked up, her voice barely a whisper. "And if we say no? What happens then?"

Mira took a deep breath, her expression softening. "If you say no, we respect your decision. We won't proceed with the serum without your consent. We'll go back to the drawing board, continue our research, and try to find another solution. But... I won't lie to you. Without these antibodies, our chances of creating an effective cure are slim."

The group fell silent once more, each individual lost in their thoughts, their faces etched with the weight of the choice that lay before them. Mira felt her heart break as she watched them, knowing that she was asking them to make an impossible decision, a sacrifice that went beyond anything they had ever faced.

Peter finally looked up, his gaze meeting hers with a mixture of defiance and resolve. "I'll do it," he said quietly, his voice filled with a fierce determination. "If there's a chance that my blood can save lives, then I'm willing to take that risk. I survived once—I'll survive again."

One by one, the others nodded, their expressions a mixture of fear and resolve. Carla's voice was steady as she spoke, though her hands trembled. "Me too. I've lost so much already. If my antibodies can help others avoid the same fate... then it's worth it."

Mira felt a surge of emotion, a mixture of pride and sorrow as she looked at them, each one willing to make the ultimate sacrifice for the sake of humanity. They were more than just immune survivors—they were heroes, individuals who had faced unimaginable hardship and emerged stronger, braver, willing to give everything for a chance to save others.

With a heavy heart, Mira nodded, her voice filled with gratitude. "Thank you. I promise, we'll do everything we can to ensure your safety, to protect you as much as possible. This isn't a decision we take lightly, and I am deeply humbled by your courage."

As the meeting concluded and the immune survivors filed out, Mira felt the weight of their choice settle over her, a burden she would carry for the rest of her life. She knew that the path ahead would be filled with challenges, that the risks were high, and that there were no guarantees. But she also knew that she had made the right choice, that she had given them the respect and agency they deserved.

And as she returned to her lab, her mind racing with the task ahead, she felt a sense of resolve, a fierce determination to honor the sacrifices they had made. She would fight for them, for their courage, for their hope, for the future they had chosen to protect.

Chapter 15: Whispers of Resistance

Dr. Mira Kline sat at her desk in the silent glow of the lab, the walls around her seemingly closer than they had ever been. She'd always considered this lab a sanctuary, a place where the pursuit of knowledge and science could thrive untainted by the noise of the outside world. But lately, her sanctuary had started to feel like a cell, one where she had no choice but to carry out the government's orders, knowing full well the costs of defying them.

The underground resistance, once a distant rumor, had grown into a tangible force, whispering in the halls of power and sending ripples through the government's hold on the immune survivors. The resistance was no longer a mere band of immunes hiding from capture; it was an organized effort to ensure freedom, to protect those who had survived the virus from becoming pawns in the government's relentless power game. And now, Mira found herself on the edge of a decision that could turn her from a reluctant observer into a crucial ally.

A soft knock at the door broke her thoughts, and she looked up to see Jamie, her assistant and closest confidant, standing in the doorway. He had become a steadying force, an ally in her growing struggle against the forces pushing her to compromise her principles. His face was tense, his usual easygoing demeanor replaced by a look of cautious urgency.

"Mira," he began, closing the door behind him and casting a wary glance over his shoulder. "We need to talk. I... I just got word from the underground."

Mira felt a jolt of anticipation, mingled with anxiety, course through her. "What did they say?"

Jamie hesitated, as if weighing his words. "They're planning to move a large group of immunes to a new safe house on the outskirts of the city. The government's increased its sweeps, and they're worried about capture. They've asked if there's anything we can do to help ensure the group stays undetected. They need our help."

Mira's heart raced, the weight of Jamie's words settling over her. The resistance was asking for her assistance directly, a call for action that she knew would demand everything she'd been holding back. She had spent months balancing on the edge, caught between her loyalty to science and her growing commitment to the immunes' cause. And now, she was being asked to make a choice that would forever define her allegiance.

"If we help them, Jamie..." she began, her voice wavering. "We're risking everything. If Lawson finds out, if the government gets even a hint that we're involved with the underground, they'll shut us down. And it won't stop there—they'll use whatever force is necessary to stamp out the resistance."

Jamie nodded, his face filled with the same mixture of fear and determination she felt. "I know, Mira. But the underground needs us. They don't have the resources or the knowledge we do, and they're up against a government that's willing to sacrifice them in the name of control. These people are fighting for their right to exist, to live free from capture and testing."

Mira took a deep breath, her mind racing as she weighed the implications of her decision. She thought of the immune individuals she had come to know, the people who had trusted her, who had placed their lives in her hands. She thought of Peter, Carla, and the others who had risked everything to avoid becoming subjects in the government's scheme. And she knew, deep down, that she couldn't turn her back on them.

"Do we have a plan?" she asked, her voice steady despite the turmoil swirling within her.

Jamie nodded, relief flickering in his eyes. "We do. I've been working with Lila and some of the others. We've mapped out a route that should bypass the main government checkpoints. But there's a risk. We need access to certain security codes to override the tracking systems, and those codes are restricted. Only a handful of people have them."

Mira's mind raced, her pulse quickening as she considered the possibilities. "And I'm assuming Lawson is one of those people?"

Jamie nodded. "Yes. And he keeps his codes encrypted on a private server in his office. I've managed to bypass some of the basic security systems in the building, but Lawson's firewall is another story. We'd need a distraction, something big enough to draw his attention away long enough for me to get in."

Mira's heart pounded as the plan began to take shape, each piece falling into place with a dangerous clarity. She knew that what they were about to undertake would place them in direct opposition to the government, that they were stepping onto a path fraught with peril. But she also knew that they had no choice. The underground was counting on them, and if they didn't act, the government would tighten its grip, crushing the resistance before it had a chance to grow.

"We'll need to be careful," she said, her voice firm. "No unnecessary risks. If we're going to pull this off, we have to be precise, calculated. There's no room for mistakes."

Jamie nodded, his expression resolute. "Agreed. I'll set up the preliminary framework, get everything in place. If all goes well, we'll be able to secure the codes and transmit them to the underground within the next forty-eight hours."

Mira watched as Jamie left the room, her heart heavy with the weight of what they were about to do. She knew that once they crossed this line, there would be no turning back. She would be branded a traitor, a dissenter, an enemy of the state. But for the first time, she felt a sense of purpose, a fierce determination to protect the people she had come to see as family.

That night, Mira lay awake in her quarters, her mind racing with the risks and consequences of their plan. She knew that she was walking a razor's edge, that any misstep could cost her everything she had worked for. But as she thought of the underground, of the immunes who were fighting for their lives, she felt a steely resolve settle over her.

She was no longer just a scientist bound by loyalty to a corrupt government. She was an ally, a protector, a voice for those who had been silenced.

The following day, Mira and Jamie set their plan into motion. They worked in the quiet hours, careful to avoid drawing attention, their movements precise and calculated. Jamie had created a diversion, a series of small but noticeable glitches in the building's security system that would require Lawson's immediate attention.

As Jamie made his way to Lawson's office, Mira monitored the cameras from her lab, her heart pounding as she watched him move through the corridors with practiced ease. She had mapped out the security cameras' blind spots, guiding Jamie through each step, her voice steady despite the fear gnawing at her.

"Turn left," she whispered into the earpiece, her eyes locked on the screen. "There's a gap between the cameras. You'll have about ten seconds before the next rotation."

Jamie nodded, moving quickly as he slipped through the door to Lawson's office, his movements swift and silent. Mira held her breath, her fingers clenched tightly as she waited, each second stretching into an eternity.

Finally, Jamie's voice crackled through the earpiece. "I'm in. Give me a few minutes to decrypt the files."

Mira nodded, her heart pounding as she kept watch on the cameras, her gaze flickering between the monitors as she scanned for any sign of movement. She knew that their plan was precarious, that any deviation could lead to disaster. But she also knew that they had no choice. The underground was counting on them, and failure was not an option.

After what felt like an eternity, Jamie's voice came through the earpiece again, his tone laced with triumph. "I've got the codes. I'm uploading them now."

Mira exhaled, relief flooding through her as she watched the data transfer on her monitor. They had done it. The codes were in their possession, a lifeline for the underground, a chance to evade the government's relentless grip.

"Get out of there, Jamie," she whispered, her voice filled with urgency. "We don't have much time."

Jamie moved quickly, slipping out of Lawson's office and making his way back through the corridors, his steps swift and silent. Mira kept a close watch on the cameras, guiding him through each blind spot, her heart pounding with each step.

Finally, Jamie reached the lab, and Mira let out a sigh of relief as he stepped inside, a look of triumph on his face.

"We did it," he said, his voice filled with a mixture of pride and exhaustion. "The codes are secure, and the underground should be able to move without detection."

Mira nodded, her heart swelling with pride as she looked at him, her mind racing with the implications of what they had just achieved. They had taken a stand, defied the government, and given the underground a fighting chance.

But as the initial rush of victory began to fade, Mira felt a chill settle over her, a gnawing sense of unease. She knew that their actions would not go unnoticed, that the government would retaliate with all the force at its disposal. They had crossed a line, and there would be no turning back.

Jamie seemed to sense her unease, his expression softening as he placed a hand on her shoulder. "We're in this together, Mira. Whatever comes next, we'll face it as a team."

Mira nodded, grateful for his presence, for his unwavering support. She knew that the road ahead would be fraught with danger, that their actions would have consequences. But she also knew that they had made the right choice, that they had fought for something greater than themselves.

As the night stretched on, Mira found herself filled with a newfound sense of purpose, a fierce determination to protect the underground, to stand by the people who had become her family. She had chosen her path, and there was no turning back.

For the first time, she felt truly free.

Mira spent the next day in a quiet state of vigilance, feeling the weight of their actions pressing down on her. Every step she took through the lab was accompanied by a growing sense of dread. She couldn't help but wonder if someone—anyone—knew what she and Jamie had done. She replayed the details in her mind, over and over, trying to convince herself they hadn't left any evidence, any slip-ups that might lead back to them.

As she worked, she noticed the small yet unmistakable signs of government tightening its grip around the facility. There were new security checkpoints, guards she hadn't seen before, and a more frequent, watchful presence from Colonel Lawson. It was clear that the higher-ups suspected something, or at least sensed that control was slipping.

Mira's breath caught when Lawson himself appeared in her lab that afternoon. He was as meticulously put together as ever, his suit pressed to perfection, every detail polished with the unmistakable touch of authority. She forced herself to focus on her work, her heart hammering as he approached.

"Dr. Kline," Lawson said smoothly, his tone even but laced with suspicion, "I understand that security updates are being implemented throughout the facility. Given recent developments, the administration wants to ensure there are no... lapses in protocol. You understand."

Mira nodded, hoping her face betrayed nothing. "Of course, Colonel. It's always better to be safe."

"Indeed," Lawson replied, his gaze narrowing as he studied her. "With everything going on out there, we can't afford any mistakes here. I'd hate to see all of your hard work jeopardized by... distractions."

The comment was subtle, but the meaning wasn't lost on her. Mira forced herself to remain calm, meeting his gaze with as much composure as she could muster. "I appreciate your concern, Colonel. I assure you, my focus remains on the research."

Lawson held her gaze for a moment longer, as if trying to gauge the sincerity in her words. Finally, he gave a tight smile, a gesture that held no warmth. "Good to hear, Dr. Kline. Let's keep it that way."

As he walked away, Mira let out a breath she hadn't realized she was holding, her mind racing with the implications of their conversation. Lawson was watching her, scrutinizing her every move. She knew that any misstep could lead to disaster, and the tension of maintaining the facade was beginning to wear on her.

That evening, as the lab emptied and the lights dimmed, Mira met Jamie in a small, secluded storage room near the back of the facility. It was one of the few places where they could speak without fear of being overheard, a sanctuary where they could plan, regroup, and brace themselves for whatever came next.

Jamie looked exhausted, his face drawn and pale, yet his eyes held a spark of defiance, a quiet resolve that mirrored her own.

"He knows something, Jamie," Mira said, her voice barely a whisper. "Lawson's been watching me, and I think he suspects we're hiding something. We have to be careful. One slip, and it's over."

Jamie nodded, his expression somber. "I know. I've tightened the security on our communications with the underground, and I've rerouted the signals through multiple channels. If anyone tries to trace them, they'll hit a wall. But we need to stay vigilant. Any misstep, any sign of interference, and they'll come down on us hard."

Mira's mind churned with the weight of their situation, her heart pounding as she considered the risks they were taking. "We can't stop now," she said firmly. "The underground is counting on us. They're moving more people out of the city tonight, and they need every bit of support we can offer."

Jamie's gaze softened, his admiration clear. "You're doing the right thing, Mira. This isn't just about survival anymore—it's about freedom. About giving people a chance to live without fear."

Mira nodded, feeling a surge of determination settle over her. She had chosen her path, a path that defied the government's grip, a path that placed loyalty to the people over loyalty to power. And she would see it through, no matter the cost.

Later that night, Mira waited by the secure terminal in her lab, her hands trembling slightly as she activated the encrypted line to the underground. The familiar flicker of the screen settled her nerves, and she exhaled, waiting for the signal to connect.

The screen brightened, revealing Lila's face, framed in shadows. She looked tired, the strain of her position evident, but her expression was resolute. They'd had several conversations now, enough that a sense of cautious trust had developed between them—a trust Mira knew was as fragile as it was essential.

"Dr. Kline," Lila greeted her, nodding slightly. "We received the codes. They worked perfectly. We were able to move nearly thirty immunes out of the city last night without detection. I... we couldn't have done it without you."

Mira felt a pang of relief, tempered by the weight of what their success meant. "I'm glad to hear it, Lila. But we need to be cautious. Lawson is tightening security here. He suspects there's a leak, and he won't stop until he finds it."

Lila's face darkened, her gaze sharpening. "Then we'll have to move faster. The government is cracking down harder every day, and we're running out of time. More immunes are arriving every night, and it's only a matter of time before they overwhelm us."

Mira nodded, her mind racing as she considered their options. She knew that the underground was growing, that more and more people were fleeing the government's reach, desperate for a chance to live freely. But with every new arrival, the risks multiplied, the chance of discovery looming ever closer.

"I'll do what I can," she promised, her voice steady. "I have access to some medical supplies, vaccines, things that could help your people. I'll try to divert some shipments, but it has to be subtle. If they notice any discrepancies, it could put everything at risk."

Lila's expression softened, gratitude flickering in her eyes. "Thank you, Mira. I know you're taking a risk to help us. But you're giving people a chance—a chance they wouldn't have without you."

Mira felt a surge of pride and humility, a sense of purpose that had been absent for so long. She had chosen this path not out of duty, but out of conviction, out of a fierce commitment to protect those who had been cast aside, to fight for the freedom they deserved.

As their conversation ended, Mira leaned back in her chair, her mind racing with plans, strategies, contingencies. She knew that the road ahead would be treacherous, that the government's grasp was tightening, that Lawson's suspicions were growing by the day. But she also knew that she would not back down, that she would continue to stand by the underground, to protect the people she had come to see as allies, as family.

In the days that followed, Mira and Jamie worked tirelessly to support the underground, diverting supplies, creating new codes, forging documents to help them evade capture. Each move was a delicate balance, a dance of deception and survival that required precision, patience, and nerves of steel.

They worked in secret, speaking in hushed tones, their actions masked beneath layers of encryption and security protocols. But despite their precautions, Mira could feel the walls closing in, could sense the growing tension that threatened to erupt at any moment.

One evening, as Mira was finishing up her work, she noticed a shadow at the door. She looked up to see Peter, his face drawn but his eyes fierce with determination.

"Mira," he said, his voice low but resolute. "We need to talk."

She motioned for him to enter, her heart pounding as he closed the door behind him.

"I heard about the supplies," he began, his gaze steady. "About the help you've been giving to the underground. I know what you're risking, and I... I wanted to thank you. You're doing something that none of us could do alone."

Mira felt a wave of emotion, a mixture of pride and gratitude as she looked at him. "I'm not doing this alone, Peter. You're all part of this fight. And it's people like you who inspire me to keep going, to keep pushing, no matter the risks."

Peter nodded, his expression softening. "Then let's keep pushing. Let's keep fighting. Because as long as we stand together, we have a chance. We have a chance to build something better."

Mira felt a surge of hope, a fierce resolve that burned within her, fueling her determination. She had chosen her side, had committed herself to the resistance, to the people who had been silenced, oppressed, cast aside. And as long as she had breath in her body, she would fight for their freedom, for their right to live without fear.

The resistance was no longer just a whisper—it was a force, a beacon of hope in a world darkened by control and corruption. And Mira knew that she would stand by them, that she would give everything she had to protect them, to see their dream of freedom become a reality.

As she and Peter left the lab that night, stepping into the shadows, Mira felt a sense of peace, a sense of purpose that carried her forward, a strength that defied the odds, that refused to be silenced.

The resistance was growing, and Mira was no longer a reluctant ally. She was a soldier in their fight, a voice for their cause, a defender of their freedom.

And she would not stop until they were free.

Chapter 16: Family Ties

Dr. Mira Kline sat alone in her office, the soft hum of the lab's machinery a familiar yet distant noise in her ears. She had spent years surrounded by data, scanning genetic codes, running tests, analyzing sequences—always in pursuit of answers, solutions, cures. But today, the numbers on her screen weren't just numbers. They were a doorway into something much deeper, something personal that she hadn't anticipated.

It started with a single genetic marker, one she had seen before but hadn't fully connected. The marker was distinct, an anomaly that she had come to recognize as a characteristic trait in the immune population. As part of her research, Mira had examined dozens of samples from immune individuals, but this time, the data struck her differently. A second marker, intertwined with the immune trait, glowed on her screen, and her heart raced as she processed what it meant.

The anomaly was present in her own genetic code.

She scanned the sequence again, double-checking for any errors, re-running her analysis with shaking hands. But the results were clear, irrefutable. Her own DNA carried the marker she had spent years studying. It was faint, almost unnoticeable, buried within her genetic code, but it was there—proof that somewhere in her lineage, this immunity existed. This wasn't just science anymore. It was family.

Mira leaned back in her chair, her mind reeling with questions. How had she missed this? How had she overlooked something so personal, so monumental? And what did it mean for her work, her motivations, her sense of duty? She had spent her life believing that her loyalty to science, to truth, was paramount, but now she was faced with a connection she hadn't anticipated, a tie that ran deeper than any research could quantify.

Her thoughts were interrupted by a soft knock at the door. She looked up to see Jamie, his face etched with concern as he took in her expression.

"Mira, are you okay?" he asked, stepping into the room. "You look like you've seen a ghost."

Mira managed a faint smile, though her mind was still spinning. "I think I have, Jamie. I just... I found something in the data. Something personal."

Jamie's eyes widened, a flicker of understanding crossing his face. "Personal? You mean... related to you?"

Mira nodded, her voice barely above a whisper. "Yes. I ran a routine genetic scan, just cross-referencing some markers in the immune population. And I found... I found the same markers in my own DNA. It's faint, but it's there. I'm... somehow, I'm connected to them."

Jamie's expression softened, a mixture of sympathy and curiosity in his eyes. "Mira, that's... incredible. It means that you have a direct link to the immunity we've been studying. Maybe someone in your family was immune, someone who passed it down."

Mira's mind raced, memories surfacing of her family, her childhood, the stories her parents had told her about their relatives. She had grown up in a small town, raised by parents who had always encouraged her curiosity, her drive for knowledge. They had spoken fondly of her grandparents, her ancestors who had lived through plagues, pandemics, hardship, but she had never imagined that their resilience might be more than just a story.

"I don't know what it means," she admitted, her voice filled with a mixture of awe and trepidation. "But I can't ignore it. This connection... it changes things. It changes everything."

Jamie placed a reassuring hand on her shoulder. "Maybe this is why you've felt such a strong pull to protect them, to find a solution that respects their autonomy. It's not just about science for you, Mira. It's family."

Mira nodded, feeling the truth of his words settle over her. She had always been driven by a sense of duty, a fierce commitment to ethical research, but now she understood that her dedication went deeper than she had realized. She wasn't just protecting the immune population out of principle; she was fighting for her own family, for the legacy that had been passed down to her, a legacy of survival, resilience, and hope.

But with that realization came a new weight, a responsibility that felt both empowering and terrifying. She knew that her connection to the immune population could be both a strength and a vulnerability, a bond that would drive her to protect them but also place her in greater danger. If Lawson or the government discovered her link to the immunes, they could use it against her, leverage her connection to manipulate her work, her loyalty.

She looked at Jamie, a steely determination settling over her. "We can't tell anyone about this. If the government finds out, if Lawson finds out, they'll use it against me. They'll use my family as a bargaining chip."

Jamie nodded, his expression serious. "I won't breathe a word of it, Mira. Your secret is safe with me."

Mira felt a surge of gratitude, a sense of relief that she wasn't alone in this. She knew that Jamie was more than just a colleague—he was her ally, her confidant, someone who would stand by her even in the face of impossible odds.

But as she looked at the data on her screen, the reality of her discovery settled over her like a shroud. She was connected to the immune population, bound by a shared heritage, a shared resilience. And now, more than ever, she was determined to protect them, to ensure that their lives, their freedom, were not sacrificed in the name of science or control.

The following days passed in a blur of research, meetings, and careful planning. Mira threw herself into her work, her resolve strengthened by her newfound connection to the immune population. She spent hours studying the genetic markers, mapping out the family lines, tracing the history of immunity that ran through her own blood.

She found herself immersed in the stories of the immune survivors, their struggles, their triumphs, each one a testament to the strength and resilience that had been passed down through generations. And as she read their stories, she felt a growing sense of responsibility, a fierce determination to protect them, to honor the legacy that had been entrusted to her.

But the closer she got to the truth, the more dangerous her work became. Lawson's presence in the lab grew more frequent, his questions more pointed, his scrutiny more intense. It was clear that he suspected something, that he sensed the shift in her motivations, her loyalties.

One evening, as Mira was finishing up her work, Lawson appeared at her door, his expression unreadable as he stepped into her office.

"Dr. Kline," he began, his tone smooth but laced with a quiet menace. "I've noticed that your research has taken an... interesting turn. Your focus on the immune population, on the family connections... it's intriguing."

Mira felt a chill run down her spine, her heart pounding as she met his gaze. She knew that Lawson was skilled at reading people, at detecting the smallest hints of deception, and she forced herself to remain calm, to betray nothing.

"My research has always been focused on the immune population," she replied evenly. "I'm simply trying to understand the factors that contribute to their resilience, to find patterns that might lead us to a cure."

Lawson's lips curved into a thin smile, his eyes narrowing. "Of course. But I can't help but wonder if there's something more to it, something... personal. You seem particularly invested in this project, Dr. Kline. More so than your usual work."

Mira felt her pulse quicken, her mind racing as she considered her response. She knew that she was treading on dangerous ground, that any hint of vulnerability could be used against her. But she also knew that she couldn't afford to show weakness, to let Lawson see the fear that lurked beneath her calm exterior.

"I'm invested because this research has the potential to save lives," she said firmly. "It's my duty as a scientist to pursue every possible avenue, to explore every connection. That's all."

Lawson studied her for a moment, his gaze calculating, as if weighing her words for any sign of deception. Finally, he gave a curt nod, though the suspicion in his eyes remained.

"Very well, Dr. Kline. But remember—your loyalty is to the government, to the people who fund this research. Any deviation from that loyalty will be... severely punished."

With that, he turned and left, leaving Mira alone in the dimly lit room, her heart pounding with a mixture of fear and defiance. She knew that Lawson's threat was real, that he would stop at nothing to maintain control over the lab, the research, and everyone within its walls.

But she also knew that she couldn't back down, that her connection to the immune population was more than just a genetic marker. It was a bond, a legacy, a responsibility that she was determined to honor, no matter the cost.

That night, Mira lay awake in her quarters, her mind racing with the weight of her discovery, the choices that lay before her. She thought of her family, her ancestors who had survived against impossible odds, who had passed down their resilience, their strength, to her. She thought of the immune survivors she had come to know, people who had become more than just subjects, who had become a part of her own story, her own journey.

And she knew, with a certainty that settled deep within her, that she would protect them. She would stand by them, fight for their freedom, their right to live without fear or control. She would honor the legacy that had been entrusted to her, a legacy of survival, of hope, of resistance.

For the first time, her fight was personal, a battle not just for science or ethics but for family, for the people who shared her blood, her history. And she would see it through to the end, no matter the risks, no matter the cost.

As dawn broke, Mira rose from her bed, her mind clear, her heart filled with a fierce determination. She was ready to face whatever challenges lay ahead, to stand against those who sought to control her, her work, her family.

The resistance was growing, and Mira knew that she was part of something greater than herself—a movement, a legacy, a fight for freedom that would not be silenced.

And she would not rest until the people she loved, the people she had vowed to protect, were free.

Chapter 17: The Shadow Plague

The alarm echoed through the sterile hallways of the research facility, piercing the silence and sending a wave of unease through the corridors. Dr. Mira Kline jolted awake from her desk, where she'd drifted off after a long night of studying immunity markers. The alarm had never sounded like this before—a low, insistent blare that signaled something beyond routine.

Jamie burst into her office, his face pale and eyes wide with panic. "Mira," he said, barely catching his breath, "it's happening again. There's a second wave... a mutation."

Mira's heart sank, dread pooling in her stomach as she processed his words. She had known the pathogen was capable of mutating, had warned her colleagues that a second wave was a possibility, but she hadn't anticipated it happening so soon, and she hadn't expected it to be this severe.

"How bad is it?" she asked, standing up and grabbing her lab coat, already in motion toward the main lab.

"It's worse than we've ever seen," Jamie replied, his voice thick with anxiety. "Reports are coming in from all over. The mutation is spreading faster than the original strain, and this time... the immunity markers don't seem to be protecting people. Survivors of the first wave are falling ill again, and the symptoms are even more intense."

Mira's blood ran cold as she absorbed the implications. If the immunity markers weren't effective against this mutated strain, it meant that her research—everything she had worked for—was back at square one. And the people who had trusted her, who had relied on their immunity for survival, were now more vulnerable than ever.

As they entered the main lab, Mira was met with the sight of her team scrambling to analyze samples, their faces etched with fear and exhaustion. Data streamed across screens, a chaotic blend of numbers and charts that painted a picture of the devastation unfolding outside their walls.

Colonel Lawson stood in the center of the room, his expression grim as he spoke with one of the lab's epidemiologists. When he saw Mira and Jamie enter, he approached them, his gaze hard and unyielding.

"Dr. Kline," he began, his voice laced with urgency, "we have a crisis on our hands. The pathogen has mutated into a more virulent strain, and it's spreading faster than we can track. We need answers, and we need them now. You and your team are to drop everything and focus on containing this mutation."

Mira's mind raced, her thoughts a whirlwind of fear and determination. She had always known that her work was high-stakes, that the pathogen was unpredictable. But now, faced with a mutation that threatened to undo all her efforts, she felt the weight of responsibility pressing down on her like never before.

"We need to isolate the mutation," she replied, her voice steady despite the turmoil within her. "If we can understand how it's changed, we might be able to develop a treatment that can target both strains."

Lawson nodded, his expression dark. "You'd better be right, Dr. Kline. If we can't stop this mutation, there won't be anyone left to save."

As he walked away, Mira turned to Jamie, her resolve hardening. "Let's get to work. We're going to need as many samples as we can get, and we'll need to run a full genetic analysis on each one. If there's any pattern, any clue to how the mutation is spreading, we have to find it."

Jamie nodded, his face set with determination as he moved to gather the necessary equipment. Mira felt a surge of gratitude for his presence, his unwavering loyalty, even in the face of such overwhelming odds. Together, they had faced countless challenges, but this was unlike anything they had ever encountered.

Hours passed in a blur of testing, analysis, and consultation with her team. The lab was filled with a tense, focused silence, broken only by the occasional click of a keyboard or the hum of the machinery. Mira worked tirelessly, her mind laser-focused as she pored over the data, searching for any indication of what had caused the mutation.

As she analyzed the samples, she noticed a disturbing pattern emerging. The mutated strain wasn't just a simple variation of the original—it was a complete restructuring of the pathogen's genetic makeup. It seemed to be targeting different markers, bypassing the immune system's defenses and attacking the body with an intensity that left little chance for survival.

She felt a chill as she realized the implications. This mutation wasn't random. It was as if the pathogen had adapted, learning from the immune responses of the survivors and evolving to become even deadlier. The idea sent a shiver down her spine, the notion that the virus was somehow "learning," adapting to each new line of defense they threw at it.

"Mira," Jamie said, his voice breaking through her thoughts. "Look at this."

He handed her a report, his face pale as he pointed to a series of numbers on the screen. "The rate of transmission... it's exponential. This mutation isn't just spreading—it's replicating at a rate five times faster than the original strain. If we don't contain this soon, it will overrun the population in a matter of weeks."

Mira's hands shook as she held the report, her mind reeling with the implications. The pathogen wasn't just mutating; it was evolving at a pace they couldn't keep up with. And if they didn't act quickly, it would be unstoppable.

"Jamie," she said, her voice filled with urgency, "we need to isolate the source of this mutation. There has to be a catalyst, something that triggered this change. If we can find it, we might be able to reverse-engineer a treatment."

Jamie nodded, his expression resolute as he moved to gather more data. Mira's mind raced as she considered their options, each one more daunting than the last. She knew that they were working against time, that every second counted. And yet, as she looked at the data streaming across her screen, she couldn't shake the feeling that they were dealing with something far more complex, far more dangerous, than she had ever imagined.

For the next 48 hours, Mira and her team worked tirelessly, pushing their bodies and minds to the limit as they raced against the clock. They ran tests, analyzed samples, and pored over every piece of data they could find, searching for any clue, any anomaly that might explain the mutation's origins.

It was during the early hours of the third day that Mira made a breakthrough. She had been analyzing a set of samples from survivors who had recently been infected with the mutated strain when she noticed something unusual. The mutation seemed to be concentrated in individuals who had received a specific form of treatment during the first wave—an experimental antiviral that had been administered to high-risk patients.

Mira's heart raced as she realized what this meant. The mutation hadn't occurred randomly; it had been triggered by the very treatments they had used to combat the virus. In their efforts to fight the pathogen, they had inadvertently created a strain that was resistant to their own defenses, a strain that was now spreading with devastating speed.

"Jamie," she said, her voice barely above a whisper. "We caused this. The treatments we used during the first wave—they triggered the mutation."

Jamie's face went pale as he absorbed her words, a look of horror crossing his features. "You mean... we're responsible for this second wave?"

Mira nodded, her heart heavy with guilt. "Yes. The antiviral treatments were effective against the original strain, but they put selective pressure on the pathogen, forcing it to evolve. This mutation... it's our doing."

Jamie sank into a chair, his face buried in his hands. "All those people... the ones we thought we were helping... we made things worse."

Mira felt a surge of despair, a wave of guilt that threatened to overwhelm her. She had dedicated her life to helping others, to finding solutions, but now she was faced with the reality that her actions had contributed to this crisis. And yet, she knew that she couldn't afford to dwell on her guilt. There were lives at stake, and if they didn't act quickly, the mutation would spread unchecked.

"Jamie," she said, her voice filled with quiet resolve. "We can't change what happened. But we can still make this right. We have to find a way to counteract the mutation, to develop a treatment that can stop it in its tracks."

Jamie looked up at her, his expression filled with a mixture of determination and regret. "You're right, Mira. We can't give up now. We owe it to those people to fix this."

Together, they worked tirelessly, pushing themselves to the brink as they searched for a solution. Mira knew that the odds were against them, that the mutation was spreading faster than they could keep up with. But she also knew that she couldn't afford to give up, that she had a responsibility to the people she had tried to help, to the immune survivors who had trusted her, to the memory of those who had already been lost.

As the days passed, Mira and Jamie delved deeper into their research, exploring every possible avenue, every potential treatment that might counteract the mutation. They tested compounds, ran simulations, and consulted with experts from around the world, piecing together a plan that might, just might, stop the mutation in its tracks.

But as they neared the end of their resources, Mira felt a growing sense of despair. The mutation was relentless, adapting to each new treatment they devised, outpacing their efforts at every turn. And as she looked at the data on her screen, she felt the weight of failure pressing down on her, a sense of hopelessness that threatened to consume her.

It was during one of these dark moments, as she sat alone in the lab, that a thought struck her—a glimmer of hope, a possibility that she had overlooked. The mutation was adaptive, evolving in response to the treatments they had used. But what if they could create a treatment that adapted just as quickly, a compound that could change with the pathogen, mimicking its evolution and countering each mutation in real-time?

The idea was radical, unprecedented, but as Mira considered the implications, she felt a surge of hope. If they could create a treatment that was as adaptable as the pathogen itself, they might be able to stay one step ahead, to contain the mutation and prevent it from spreading further.

"Jamie," she called, her voice filled with excitement. "I think I have an idea—a treatment that adapts with the mutation, one that could counter each new strain as it evolves."

Jamie looked at her, his eyes filled with a mixture of hope and skepticism. "Is that even possible?"

Mira nodded, her mind racing as she outlined her plan. "It's a long shot, and it would require resources we don't have. But if we can create a compound that responds to the pathogen's genetic markers, one that changes with each new mutation, we might be able to stop it."

Jamie's face lit up with determination, and together, they set to work, developing a prototype for the adaptive treatment. They knew that the odds were against them, that the path they had chosen was fraught with challenges. But as they worked,

Mira felt a sense of purpose, a fierce determination to make things right, to protect the people she had vowed to help.

The next few weeks were a blur of testing, adjustments, and late nights, each step bringing them closer to a solution. They encountered setbacks, moments of doubt, but they pushed forward, driven by the knowledge that failure was not an option.

Finally, after countless hours of work, they developed a prototype—a treatment that adapted in real-time, changing with each mutation, a compound that held the potential to stop the pathogen in its tracks.

Mira held the vial in her hands, a mixture of hope and fear swirling within her as she prepared to test the treatment. She knew that the stakes were high, that the fate of countless lives depended on the success of this one, fragile compound.

As she administered the treatment, holding her breath as she watched the results unfold, Mira felt a surge of hope. This was their last chance, their final stand against the pathogen that had brought so much devastation.

And as the results appeared on the screen, a glimmer of relief, a sense of victory washed over her.

They had done it.

Chapter 18: The Immunity Blueprint

Dr. Mira Kline felt a sense of mounting excitement and trepidation as she scrolled through the latest data on her monitor. Her team had spent months working tirelessly to understand the genetic mechanisms behind immunity, analyzing every sample they could acquire from immune individuals. But now, at long last, she was staring at a breakthrough—an intricate map of the genes responsible for immunity to the pathogen, a "blueprint" encoded in the survivors' DNA.

For Mira, this was a moment she had both hoped for and feared. The implications were staggering; the blueprint held the potential to save countless lives, to develop a cure that could immunize the entire population. But the data on her screen also held a darker truth. If placed in the wrong hands, the immunity blueprint could be exploited to control the population selectively, deciding who would live and who would be left vulnerable.

Jamie, her colleague and closest confidant, entered her office, holding a stack of reports. His face was tense, though his eyes lit up when he saw her expression.

"Mira, did you finally crack it?" he asked, setting the reports aside.

Mira nodded, her gaze fixed on the screen. "We did it, Jamie. We've mapped the entire genetic structure that gives people immunity to the pathogen. It's all here—the specific genes, the markers, everything."

Jamie let out a breath, his face a mixture of relief and disbelief. "That's... incredible. This could be the answer we've been looking for. With this, we could engineer a universal cure. You've changed everything, Mira."

But Mira's excitement was tempered by a growing sense of unease. She knew that the blueprint represented more than just a scientific breakthrough—it was a tool, one that could be wielded for good or for harm. In the right hands, it could be used to save lives, to end the crisis once and for all. But in the hands of someone like Colonel Lawson or the government's higher-ups, it could become a weapon of control, a way to decide who would be immune and who would remain vulnerable.

"Jamie," she said, her voice quiet, "this data is powerful—too powerful. If we aren't careful, it could be used to control people, to decide who gets immunity and who doesn't. This blueprint could become a weapon."

Jamie's expression grew serious, his gaze flickering with understanding. "You're right. We can't just hand this over to the government. If Lawson gets his hands on this... he'll use it to solidify their grip on the population, to control who survives. We've seen how far they're willing to go for power."

Mira nodded, her mind racing as she considered their options. She knew that hiding the blueprint was impossible;

once the data was on the servers, the government would have access to it. But if she could encode it, encrypt it in a way that only she and Jamie could decipher, they might be able to buy themselves some time, to ensure that the blueprint wasn't used for nefarious purposes.

"We need to encrypt this data," she said, her voice filled with determination. "We'll create a separate, hidden file with the immunity blueprint and password-protect it with the highest security protocols. And we'll keep the key to ourselves. No one else can know."

Jamie nodded, his expression resolute. "Agreed. If we keep the blueprint hidden, we can control who has access to it, ensure that it's used for the right reasons. But we'll need to be careful. Lawson will be watching us closely."

They set to work, moving quickly to encrypt the data, their hands flying over the keyboards as they encoded the blueprint with multiple layers of security. They knew that this was a risky move, that hiding the data could be considered an act of defiance. But they also knew that they couldn't allow the blueprint to be exploited, that they had a responsibility to protect it.

As they finished encrypting the file, Mira felt a sense of relief mingled with a lingering tension. They had safeguarded the blueprint, had taken steps to ensure that it wouldn't fall into the wrong hands. But she knew that this was only the beginning, that the government would stop at nothing to obtain the data they had worked so hard to protect.

Over the next few days, Mira and Jamie continued their work in secret, developing a plan to use the blueprint in a way that would benefit the immune population without sacrificing their autonomy. They knew that a cure was within reach, that they could use the immunity blueprint to engineer a serum that would provide protection against both the original pathogen and its deadly mutation.

But as they worked, Mira felt the weight of her decision pressing down on her. She was walking a fine line, balancing her loyalty to science and her commitment to ethical responsibility. She knew that one misstep could expose their secret, that Lawson's surveillance was unrelenting, and that any sign of resistance could lead to disastrous consequences.

One evening, as Mira was wrapping up her work, Colonel Lawson entered her lab, his expression as cold and unyielding as ever. Mira forced herself to remain calm, her heart pounding as he approached, his gaze sharp and assessing.

"Dr. Kline," Lawson began, his tone laced with suspicion. "I understand you've made progress on the immunity research. Care to share the details?"

Mira met his gaze, carefully schooling her expression. "We've mapped the immunity markers, Colonel. We're close to identifying a viable treatment. But the research is complex, and we're still refining the process."

Lawson's eyes narrowed, his voice low and calculated. "I trust you're aware of the importance of transparency, Dr. Kline. The government has invested significant resources in this research, and we expect full access to all data—immediately."

Mira felt a surge of anger, her resolve hardening as she maintained her composure. She knew that Lawson wasn't asking for transparency out of scientific curiosity; he wanted control, a way to weaponize her findings.

"Of course, Colonel," she replied smoothly. "We're compiling a report on our progress, and you'll have access to all pertinent data as soon as it's ready. But I caution you that the blueprint is delicate—any misuse could lead to unintended consequences."

Lawson's gaze remained fixed on her, his expression unreadable. "Unintended consequences? Or are you hiding something, Dr. Kline?"

Mira forced herself to remain calm, her pulse quickening as she met his gaze. "I'm simply advising caution, Colonel. The immunity blueprint is complex, and any attempts to alter it could jeopardize its efficacy."

Lawson studied her for a moment longer, his gaze filled with an unspoken warning. "See that you remember your place, Dr. Kline. The government expects results, and we will not tolerate insubordination. The immunity research is our top priority."

With that, he turned and left, leaving Mira alone in the dimly lit lab, her heart racing with a mixture of fear and defiance. She knew that Lawson was growing suspicious, that he wouldn't hesitate to tighten his grip if he sensed resistance. But she also knew that she couldn't back down, that her responsibility was to protect the blueprint and ensure that it was used for the right reasons.

As the days passed, Mira and Jamie continued their work, operating in secret, their every move carefully calculated to avoid detection. They knew that time was running out, that Lawson's surveillance was relentless, and that any sign of defiance could lead to catastrophic consequences.

One night, as they were finalizing the serum prototype, Mira received a message from the underground. Lila, one of the leaders of the resistance, had contacted her, requesting an urgent meeting. Mira felt a surge of anticipation mingled with apprehension. She knew that the underground was growing stronger, that their influence was spreading, and that they represented the only hope of protecting the immunity blueprint from exploitation.

She met Lila in a secluded part of the city, away from prying eyes and government surveillance. Lila's face was etched with determination, her gaze steady as she greeted Mira.

"Thank you for meeting me, Dr. Kline," Lila said, her voice low. "We've heard about your progress with the immunity blueprint. We know what it means."

Mira nodded, her mind racing as she considered the implications of Lila's words. She knew that the underground had access to information the government didn't, that they were more aware of the stakes than most people realized.

"The blueprint is powerful," Mira replied quietly. "But it's also dangerous. If the government gains control of it, they'll use it to control the population, to decide who survives and who doesn't. We can't let that happen."

Lila nodded, her expression fierce. "That's why we need your help. The underground has resources, contacts, people willing to fight for their freedom. If we can work together, we can ensure that the blueprint is used ethically, that it protects the immune population rather than enslaving them."

Mira felt a surge of hope, a sense of purpose that had been missing for so long. She knew that joining forces with the underground was a risk, that it would place her in direct opposition to the government. But she also knew that it was the only way to protect the blueprint, to ensure that her work wasn't exploited for control.

"I'll help you," Mira said, her voice filled with determination. "But we have to be careful. Lawson is watching me closely, and any sign of resistance will put us all at risk."

Lila nodded, her gaze filled with gratitude. "We understand the risks, Dr. Kline. But we're prepared to fight. This is about more than survival—it's about freedom, about protecting our right to live without fear."

Together, they devised a plan to protect the blueprint, to ensure that it was used to benefit the immune population rather than oppress them. Mira knew that the road ahead would be treacherous, that they were walking a fine line between freedom and control. But she also knew that she had chosen her side, that her loyalty was to the people who had trusted her, who had placed their lives in her hands.

In the days that followed, Mira and Jamie worked tirelessly to implement their plan, encrypting the blueprint with additional layers of security, creating backups, and establishing secure channels with the underground. They knew that their actions were risky, that any misstep could expose their secret and lead to dire consequences.

But they also knew that they were fighting for something greater than themselves, for a future where the immunity blueprint was a tool of liberation rather than oppression.

And as Mira looked at the blueprint on her screen, a sense of peace settled over her. She had made her choice, had committed herself to the fight, to the people who had become her family.

The immunity blueprint was more than just a scientific breakthrough—it was a symbol of hope, of resilience, of the human spirit. And as long as she had breath in her body, Mira would protect it, would stand by the people who had trusted her, would fight for their right to live freely.

Chapter 19: Sacrifice and Redemption

Dr. Mira Kline stood in the sterile silence of her lab, staring at the vial in her hand. The serum inside represented years of work, countless hours of research, and a path forward—a cure. But this wasn't just any cure. It was a selective solution, one that could target the immune markers she had painstakingly mapped, granting immunity to specific individuals while leaving others vulnerable.

It was a tool of unimaginable power, a gift that could save millions, but also a weapon that could control them. In the wrong hands, it could cement a hierarchy, deciding who would live and who would face the pathogen without protection. The thought sent a chill through her, and for the first time, she felt the full weight of what she had created.

Jamie entered the lab, his face etched with concern as he noticed the vial in her hand. He had been by her side through every discovery, every setback, and every moral crossroad, but Mira could tell he sensed something different in her this time.

"Mira," he said gently, stepping closer, "is that it?"

Mira nodded, unable to tear her gaze from the shimmering liquid in the vial. "This is it, Jamie. The cure. But it's more than that. It's a choice. I don't know if I can go through with it."

Jamie watched her carefully, understanding the storm of emotions behind her eyes. "You've spent years fighting for this moment. But I know what you're thinking. Once you release it, we lose control of how it's used. And we both know how Colonel Lawson would use it."

Mira closed her eyes, the tension building in her chest. She could still feel Lawson's presence hovering like a shadow, his words echoing in her mind. He had made it clear that he wanted absolute control over the immunity blueprint, that he would use it to secure the government's power over the immune population. If she handed the serum over to him, she might be saving lives in the short term, but she would be condemning others to a life of control, surveillance, and exploitation.

"What do we do, Jamie?" Mira whispered, her voice barely audible. "I created this to save lives, to end the suffering, but... what if releasing it just gives Lawson and the government more power?"

Jamie took a deep breath, his gaze steady. "You have to ask yourself what matters most. Are you willing to sacrifice your principles, your vision, for the sake of immediate relief? Or are you willing to take a stand, to risk everything to protect those who might be exploited?"

Mira felt a surge of emotion, a wave of guilt and responsibility washing over her. She had dedicated her life to science, to helping others, but now she was faced with a choice that went beyond science, beyond her duty as a doctor. This was a decision about power, control, and the very essence of freedom. She had the power to create a cure, but did she have the right to decide how it was used?

She looked at Jamie, her voice filled with desperation. "If I release the selective cure, I'm putting people's lives in Lawson's hands. I'd be giving him the power to decide who lives and who doesn't. But if I don't release it... people will continue to suffer. More will die."

Jamie reached out, placing a reassuring hand on her shoulder. "You don't have to make this decision alone, Mira. We can find another way. Maybe there's a solution we haven't considered yet, a way to release the cure without handing over control."

Mira's mind raced, her thoughts swirling as she considered his words. She knew that Jamie was right, that there had to be another way, a way to protect the people she cared about without sacrificing her integrity. But the clock was ticking, and every moment she hesitated, more lives were at risk.

As they stood in silence, a soft beep sounded from Mira's computer. She turned to see a message flashing on the screen—a message from Lila, one of the leaders of the underground resistance.

"Dr. Kline," the message read, "we have a situation. The government is planning a raid on our safe houses. They're looking for immune survivors. We need your help."

Mira's heart pounded as she read the message, her mind racing as she processed the implications. The government was closing in on the underground, on the very people she had sworn to protect. If they were captured, they would become test subjects, pawns in the government's quest for control. And she knew that her decision about the cure would directly impact their fate.

She looked at Jamie, her voice filled with urgency. "They're going after the underground, Jamie. If they capture those people, they'll use them to justify taking control of the cure, to make sure that only those loyal to the government receive immunity."

Jamie's face hardened, his gaze filled with determination. "Then we can't let that happen. We have to warn them, to give them a chance to escape. And we have to find a way to release the cure in a way that protects them."

Mira nodded, her resolve strengthening. She knew that this was her chance, her opportunity to make a difference, to stand up for the people she had come to see as family. She had spent her life fighting for the truth, for justice, and now she was being called to take a stand, to protect those who couldn't protect themselves.

They worked quickly, devising a plan to warn the underground and to buy themselves time to distribute the cure. Mira knew that this was a dangerous game, that any misstep could lead to disaster. But she also knew that she couldn't afford to back down, that she had a responsibility to the people who had placed their trust in her.

As they prepared to leave, Mira slipped the vial of the selective cure into her pocket, a reminder of the choice she still had to make. She didn't know what the future held, but she knew that she would do everything in her power to protect the people she loved, to ensure that the cure was used for good rather than control.

They moved swiftly, navigating the city's underground network, their every step filled with purpose and urgency. Mira felt the weight of her decision pressing down on her, the knowledge that she was walking a fine line between hope and despair, between sacrifice and redemption.

When they reached the underground safe house, Mira was met by Lila and a small group of immune survivors. Their faces were etched with fear and exhaustion, but their eyes held a spark of determination, a fierce resilience that reminded Mira of why she had chosen this path.

"Dr. Kline," Lila said, her voice filled with gratitude, "thank you for coming. We heard about the government's plans, and we knew we couldn't do this without your help."

Mira nodded, her gaze steady. "We don't have much time. They're coming for you, and they won't stop until they have what they want. But I'm not going to let that happen. I've developed a cure, but... it's a selective solution. If it falls into the wrong hands, it could be used to control who receives immunity."

Lila's expression hardened, her eyes filled with understanding. "So you're faced with a choice. Release the cure and risk exploitation, or hold onto it and risk more lives."

Mira felt a surge of guilt, a wave of responsibility that threatened to overwhelm her. "Yes. And I don't know what to do. I want to protect you, to ensure that the cure is used for good, but... I don't know if I have the right to decide."

Lila placed a hand on Mira's shoulder, her gaze filled with compassion. "Dr. Kline, you've done more for us than anyone else. You've risked everything to protect us, to fight for our freedom. But this decision... it's not yours to make alone. We're in this together, and we'll face whatever comes together."

Mira felt a sense of relief, a weight lifting from her shoulders as she realized that she wasn't alone, that she didn't have to carry this burden by herself. She had allies, people who shared her vision, her commitment to freedom and justice.

As they prepared to distribute the cure, Mira felt a surge of hope, a renewed sense of purpose. She knew that they were facing impossible odds, that the government would stop at nothing to maintain control. But she also knew that they were fighting for something greater than themselves, for a future where immunity was a right, not a privilege.

Together, they worked through the night, distributing the cure to those who needed it most, ensuring that it would be used to protect rather than control. Mira felt a sense of redemption, a feeling of peace that she had made the right choice, that she had honored her principles, her vision.

As dawn broke, Mira looked at the people around her, her heart filled with gratitude, with a fierce determination to continue the fight. She knew that this was only the beginning, that they would face more challenges, more sacrifices. But she also knew that they were stronger together, that their commitment to each other would carry them through whatever lay ahead.

Chapter 20: A New Dawn

Dr. Mira Kline stood at the edge of the dawn, watching as the first light broke across the city. The vial of the selective cure—the culmination of her life's work—felt heavy in her pocket. Around her, the city seemed quiet, almost serene, but she knew that beneath the surface lay tensions, questions, and fears that her decision would either quell or ignite.

She had spent the night in restless contemplation, turning over each consequence, weighing each possible outcome. Releasing the cure as it was—a selective, immunity-based solution—could offer salvation to millions. Yet it could also cement hierarchies of control, giving those in power the ability to decide who would be protected and who would not. She could already see how Colonel Lawson and his team would capitalize on it, using it to shape society according to their interests, making immunity a currency of power and control.

Jamie stood beside her, his gaze fixed on the horizon. He had been her unwavering ally, her moral compass through the darkness, and now he awaited her decision, ready to support her no matter the path she chose.

"Do you think we're doing the right thing, Jamie?" Mira asked, her voice barely more than a whisper.

Jamie's eyes softened, his gaze filled with understanding. "I think the right thing isn't always clear. But you've fought for people's freedom, Mira, for their right to live without fear. Whatever you decide, you've already changed lives, given people a reason to hope."

Mira nodded, the weight of his words settling over her. She knew that he was right, that she had already made a difference, but this decision—this final choice—felt like the last piece in a complex puzzle. And once placed, it would be irreversible.

Together, they turned and walked back into the lab, where the vial awaited its destiny.

The news of Mira's decision spread quickly. Within hours, it reached the ears of Colonel Lawson, whose expression darkened as he processed her actions. He had expected Mira to comply, to follow his orders without question, but he hadn't anticipated the full scope of her defiance. Mira hadn't just released the cure—she had distributed it freely, anonymously, bypassing government channels and ensuring that it reached the hands of the people most in need.

Lawson's fury was palpable, his anger seething beneath the surface as he called a meeting with the government's top officials. Mira's actions had blindsided him, undermining his authority and challenging the very power structure he had fought to uphold.

"She's jeopardized everything we've worked for," Lawson growled, his fists clenched as he addressed the room. "By distributing the cure without authorization, she's created a situation we can no longer control. Immunity should be a privilege, something we can leverage, but she's given it away as if it were her decision to make."

One of the officials, a woman with a shrewd gaze, leaned forward, her tone calm but cold. "Perhaps, Colonel, we underestimated Dr. Kline's resolve. She's clearly committed to her ideals, and she's willing to defy us to see them through."

Lawson's eyes narrowed, his voice low and menacing. "She's placed ideals above practicality, above loyalty. And now, she'll face the consequences."

Meanwhile, Mira continued her work in the lab, unaware of the storm her decision had sparked in the government's highest circles. She felt a quiet sense of purpose, a conviction that she had chosen the right path. For the first time, she felt free of the constraints that had bound her, free to pursue her vision of a world where immunity wasn't a commodity but a right—a gift that should belong to everyone, not just the privileged few.

Jamie was at her side, assisting her as they prepared additional doses, ensuring that the distribution network they had established was secure and that the cure would continue to reach the people who needed it most.

As they worked, Mira felt a surge of hope, a sense that they were standing on the brink of a new era. She knew that there would be challenges, that the government would try to regain control, but she believed that the people would rally, that they would stand together to protect their newfound freedom.

"Do you think they'll come after us?" Jamie asked quietly, his gaze steady as he looked at her.

Mira took a deep breath, her expression resolute. "Yes. They won't let this go easily. But I'm prepared to face whatever comes. We're fighting for something greater than ourselves, Jamie. And I believe that the people will stand with us."

In the weeks that followed, Mira's vision began to take shape. The cure spread throughout the population, reaching people from all walks of life, giving them a sense of security and hope that had been absent for so long. Communities began to rebuild, survivors found a renewed sense of purpose, and the fear that had gripped the city for so long began to dissipate.

But the government's response was swift and unforgiving. Lawson implemented a series of measures designed to regain control, tightening security, monitoring movements, and enforcing restrictions on those who had received the cure without authorization. He was determined to crush the rebellion Mira had ignited, to remind the people that power belonged to the government, not the individual.

Mira and Jamie continued their work in secret, coordinating with the underground, who had become their allies in the fight for freedom. They knew that the battle was far from over, that they were standing against a force that would stop at nothing to maintain control. But they also knew that they weren't alone, that they were part of a growing movement that believed in a world where immunity wasn't a privilege, but a right.

One evening, as Mira was finishing up her work, she received an urgent message from Lila, one of the leaders of the underground.

"Mira," the message read, "Lawson's forces are closing in. They're planning a raid on our safe houses, targeting the people who received the cure. We need your help."

Mira's heart raced as she read the message, her mind racing as she considered their options. She knew that this was the government's attempt to regain control, to reassert their authority by targeting the people she had sought to protect. And she knew that if they succeeded, it would send a message to the population—a warning that any defiance would be met with harsh consequences.

"We have to act," Mira said, her voice filled with urgency as she turned to Jamie. "If Lawson's forces capture the people we've helped, they'll undo everything we've worked for. They'll make an example of them."

Jamie nodded, his face set with determination. "Then we have to get to them first. We'll warn them, help them escape before the raid."

Together, they set out, navigating the city's underground network, moving swiftly and silently as they made their way to the safe houses. Mira felt a surge of adrenaline, a fierce determination to protect the people who had become her allies, her family.

When they arrived, they found Lila and a group of immune survivors, their faces etched with fear but their eyes filled with resilience.

"Dr. Kline," Lila said, her voice laced with relief, "we didn't think you'd make it in time."

Mira placed a reassuring hand on her shoulder, her gaze steady. "We're not going to let them take you. We have a plan, but we'll need everyone's cooperation."

As they coordinated the escape, Mira felt a sense of purpose, a clarity that had eluded her for so long. She was no longer just a scientist bound by duty or loyalty to a corrupt government. She was a leader, a protector, a voice for those who had been silenced.

When Lawson's forces arrived, they found the safe houses empty, the people they had sought to capture gone without a trace. Mira watched from a distance, her heart pounding with a mixture of relief and defiance. She knew that this was a victory, a small but significant blow against the forces of control and oppression.

But she also knew that it was only the beginning, that the fight for freedom was far from over.

As the weeks turned into months, Mira's movement grew, fueled by the people's desire for autonomy and the hope that she had given them. The government's grip weakened, its authority challenged by a population that had tasted freedom and refused to return to a life of fear.

Colonel Lawson's influence waned, his attempts to regain control met with resistance at every turn. Mira's vision—a society where immunity was a right, not a privilege—began to take shape, a new dawn rising over the city.

And as Mira looked out at the world she had helped to create, she felt a sense of peace, a feeling of redemption. She had faced her darkest hour, had made a choice that had reshaped the future, and she knew that she had done the right thing.

She had given the people a reason to hope, a chance to build a life free from control and fear.

It was the beginning of a new age, a world where immunity was not a tool of power but a gift, a symbol of resilience and hope.

And as the sun rose over the city, Mira knew that this was only the beginning.

Thank You for Reading

DEAR READER,

Thank you for embarking on this journey with **The Doctor's Dilemma Collection**. I truly appreciate your time, curiosity, and support in exploring the intricate world of medicine through these stories .If this book resonated with you or inspired new perspectives, please consider supporting future projects and publications. Your generous contributions make it possible to continue creating meaningful content.

Support My Work:

Venmo: @Nileshlp

Cash App: $drnileshlp

BTC

bc1qs72228z6pauw3rk9tej9f6umu4y9gz289y3cvn

ETH

0xE1DAE6F656c900a4b24257b587ac0856E1e346D2

Every bit of support goes a long way in sustaining my passion for storytelling and public health advocacy. Once again, thank you from the bottom of my heart. Your encouragement and generosity mean the world to me.

Warm regards,

Dr. Nilesh Panchal

Author and Public Health Practitioner

Don't miss out!

Visit the website below and you can sign up to receive emails whenever Dr. Nilesh Panchal publishes a new book. There's no charge and no obligation.

https://books2read.com/r/B-A-JKGNC-YFDGF

BOOKS 2 READ

Connecting independent readers to independent writers.

Did you love *Whispers of the Immune*? Then you should read *The Last Patient*[1] by Dr. Nilesh Panchal!

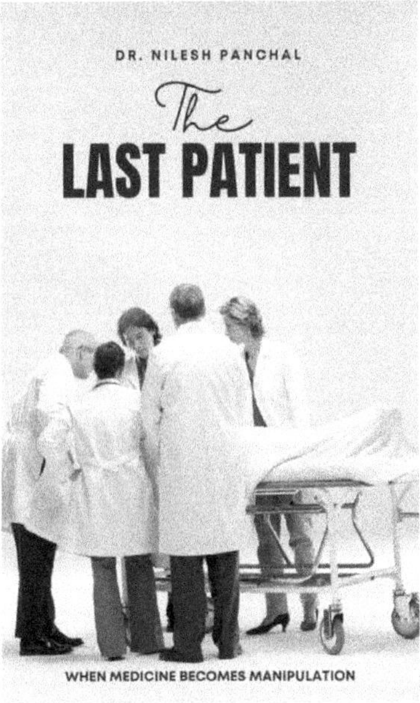

2

In ***The Last Patient***, Dr. Rahul Varma relocates to the quiet town of Hazelwood, hoping for a peaceful practice, only to uncover a chilling secret: the residents are unknowingly being used as subjects in a covert clinical trial for a new psychiatric drug. As he delves deeper, he unravels a web of deception involving the pharmaceutical company, town officials, and even some of his own patients. With mounting pressure to stay silent and his career on the line, Dr. Varma must decide whether to risk everything to expose the truth. Blending medical ethics,

---

1. https://books2read.com/u/3nPrr8
2. https://books2read.com/u/3nPrr8

small-town intrigue, and psychological suspense, *The Last Patient* is a gripping exploration of the dark side of clinical research and the moral cost of justice.

Read more at https://drmedhealth.com/.

Also by Dr. Nilesh Panchal

Clinical Trials Mastery Series
Essentials of Clinical Trials
Clinical Trials: Ethical Considerations and Regulations
Clinical Trials Design and Methodology

Mastering the FDA Approval Process
Mastering New Drug Applications A Step-by-Step Guide
Navigating ANDA: Strategies for Effective Generic Drug Approval
Mastering PMA: A Comprehensive Guide to Premarket Approval for Medical Devices

The Doctor's Dilemma Collection
A Heartbeat Away
Human Trial
The Surgeon's Dilemma
The Last Patient
The Organ Broker

The Healer's Secret
Brainwaves
Silent Invasion
Echoes in the Genome
Whispers of the Immune

Standalone
Navigating FDA Drug Approval
Healthy Habits: A Kid's Guide to Wellness
Mastering Medical Terminology
Navigating the FDA 510(k) Process
Essential First Aid: Life-Saving Techniques for Everyone

Watch for more at https://drmedhealth.com/.

About the Author

Dr. Nilesh Panchal is a distinguished Public Health Practitioner and Health Scientist with over two decades of experience, making significant contributions to the fields of infectious diseases, mental health, and public health education. Holding a DrPH in Public Health Practice, Dr. Panchal is a prolific author known for his ability to translate complex medical concepts into accessible and engaging content for a broad audience. His work, including the acclaimed series "Global Outbreaks: The Saga of Humanity's Health Battles," provides invaluable insights into the challenges posed by infectious diseases, making it an authoritative source for understanding humanity's ongoing battle against deadly pathogens. Dr. Panchal's dedication to educating the public extends to his "Mindfulness and Well-Being Series," where his compassionate and practical approach empowers readers to enhance their mental and emotional well-being.

In addition to his focus on infectious diseases and mental health, Dr. Panchal has made remarkable strides in lifestyle medicine, particularly in the prevention of diabetes. His book series "Healthy Living, Healthy Future: Diabetes Prevention Series" offers evidence-based strategies that empower individuals to make lasting lifestyle changes for a healthier, diabetes-free life. Dr. Panchal's commitment to public health is also reflected in his guide "Essential First Aid: Life-Saving Techniques for Everyone," where he provides clear, step-by-step instructions for managing emergencies. Through his extensive research, Dr. Panchal continues to be a respected voice in global health, contributing to medical journals, speaking at international conferences, and leading health innovation projects aimed at integrating AI into clinical practice. His body of work not only informs but also inspires, making a lasting impact on global health practices and public education.

Read more at https://drmedhealth.com/.

Milton Keynes UK
Ingram Content Group UK Ltd.
UKHW030854111124
451035UK00001B/52

9 798227 439963